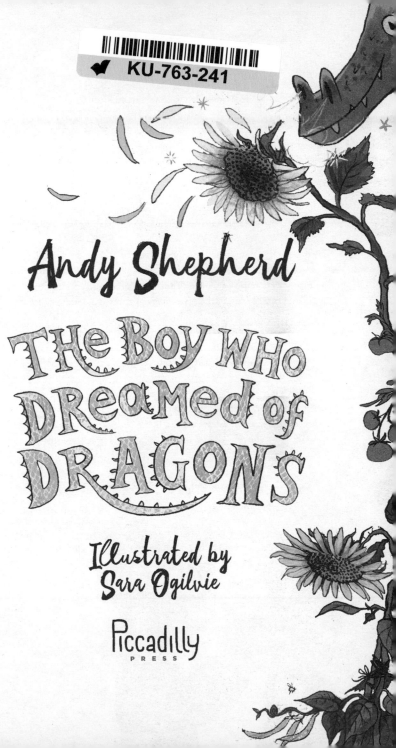

Andy Shepherd

THE BOY WHO DREAMED OF DRAGONS

Illustrated by
Sara Ogilvie

Piccadilly
PRESS

First published in Great Britain in 2020 by
PICCADILLY PRESS
80–81 Wimpole St, London W1G 9RE
Owned by Bonnier Books
Sveavägen 56, Stockholm, Sweden
www.piccadillypress.co.uk

ISBN: 978-1-84812-925-2
Also available as an ebook and in audio

Printed and bound in Great Britain by Clays Ltd, Elcograf S.p.A.

Piccadilly Press is an imprint of Bonnier Books UK
www.bonnierbooks.co.uk

For Mum, Dad and Pete
With my love and thanks always

We dream of dragons. Soaring, roaring, fire-flickering dragons. While we're tucked tight in bed, they light up our sleep. Sparking, glittering, aglow.

But dreams are only the beginning of an even greater story. And if you carry on reading, you'll discover that there's a whole lot more story still to be told.

Because the truth is, our dragons don't just visit us in our dreams.

You see, a few of us know a secret. And that secret is that some dragons grow on trees. A very special tree, which grows at the bottom of my grandad's garden, in among the brambles and nettles.

If I blurted this out to most people, right about now they'd roll their eyes and think I was joking – and that's good. Because we don't want everyone knowing about this. In fact, it means we're doing our job. Keeping the dragons safe and secret.

But how about you? Do you think I'm pulling your leg? No, I think you've got that glint in your eye, like a dragon's fiery breath sparking across your sights. And you know what? That tells me you're the right person to hear this. So, are you ready?

1
The Marshmallow
Wins It

I gripped my knees tightly to Flicker's back and wrapped my arms around his neck. A flash of colour pulsed across his scales, lighting up my hands. Red, green, indigo and bright gold. It was like there was a rainbow shooting from my fingertips, as the colour raced on towards his head.

He twisted, one diamond eye catching mine. And then we dived.

Yup! This was my life now, riding on the back of dragons!

I kept my head low and hung on, the wind tugging

at me, trying to pull me free. But there was no way I was letting go. Even though I'd left my stomach doing somersaults up there somewhere.

A roar came from behind me and I saw the golden shape of Ted's dragon, Sunny, rocketing towards us as we levelled off.

'I'm coming for you, Tomas,' Ted yelled, as they shot past. Flicker swerved to avoid the fiery blast coming from Sunny's rear end.

'Not fair,' I shouted. Flicker was fast, but he didn't stand a chance against Ted's dragon when he got one of those turbo boosts. I was beginning to think we should disqualify Ted, or at least ban Sunny from scoffing giant marshmallows before a race.

And then came the rest of the superhero squad. First Liam, riding Maxi, one hand raised, a massive grin plastered across his face. And to my left, Kat and Kai riding Crystal and Dodger, still neck and neck, their tails flicking out every so often, trying to make the other veer off course. Good. That meant they were too busy trying to beat each other to be a serious threat.

There was a rumble and Flicker opened his jaws and blue flames shot out. This race wasn't over. Not by a long shot. Flicker's wings beat hard and fast. He let out another bellow as he gained on Sunny.

Back when Flicker was only small and hiccupping sparks, I used to dream of flying, wondering what it would feel like to ride on a dragon. And now I knew. Above the clouds, arcing through the sky like a shooting star, I hollered with him.

Up here everything was so bright and clear, with the colours of the sunset lighting our way. Just us, in this brilliant moment that might last forever. Everything else hidden below.

Even at dusk, the dragons wouldn't fly down through the cloud cover until we were right over Nana and Grandad's house. The people in our village might be too wrapped up in their busy lives to notice they were living alongside small hatching dragons, but we couldn't risk someone glancing up and spotting five fully grown dragons flying over the neighbourhood!

The trouble was, if we left it too long we'd overshoot and have to double back. And then the race would be over for me and Flicker. It was all about timing it just right.

I felt myself tilt forward as Flicker flew lower.

'Not yet . . .' I whispered.

But he didn't listen. I opened my mouth, about to urge him to pull up, but then I stopped. Sometimes you just have to trust your dragon.

So I wrapped my arms around his neck and braced myself as Flicker headed straight into the billowing cloud.

The blue sparks that he blew out crackled like a tiny lightning storm. I just hoped those diamond eyes of his could see more than I could. Which was absolutely zilch.

Just when I was beginning to wonder if he'd actually got lost, he finally flew down through the cloud and we were out the other side. I couldn't help giving a whoop of delight as I shook off the water dripping from my hair.

There below us was Grandad's garden. I could see the trees with their little twinkly fairy lights sparkling through the dark, and the glittery horns of Tinkle, Lolli's dragon, lying curled beneath them. And then I spied Grandad. He was walking very slowly in a straight line, arms outstretched. I wondered what he could be doing, until I saw Lolli brandishing a stick, her other hand holding down the wobbly pirate hat that was far too big for her. She looked up and waved. Then pointed her sword away from her lily-livered captive and up to the sky. I turned just in time to see Sunny rocketing out of the cloud. Seconds later Ted was flying alongside me, grinning.

'Thought you had us there, Tomas,' he cried.

As I was about to answer I saw Lolli reach into her pocket. I grinned.

'Not over yet.' I laughed and nodded towards Lolli, who was casually hurling marshmallow after marshmallow into the air.

'Not fair,' Ted wailed, as Sunny swerved away from the finish line, all his attention on the sweet treats raining down onto the grass.

I yelled in triumph as Flicker flew over Grandad's shed in first place.

Best dragon race ever!

2
Watch Your Step!

By the time the others joined us, Ted had forgiven Sunny for his betrayal with the marshmallows and was tucking into the packet himself.

If I'm honest, there wasn't a lot of room once all the dragons had landed.

Kat laughed. 'I'm not sure they'd fit in the Dragons' Den these days.'

'Good job they've had an upgrade!' Ted said.

It was Kat who'd suggested where the dragons could stay on their visits. An old quarry a few miles away had been flooded and turned into a nature reserve. Out in the middle of the lake was a small wooded island, which had become the perfect place for the dragons to hide out.

As I stood and watched Flicker and the others soar into the sky, I wondered how long they would stay this time. Although they had only just arrived, I knew we would have them for only a few days at most, before they headed north again. After that, who knew when they'd return?

Kat, Kai and Liam headed home, but I stayed in the garden with Ted. Lolli and Grandad had planted some chilli peppers and she was whispering to the little seedlings and tickling their leaves, while he filled a can from the water butt. Once they'd finished, Grandad declared it was time for a cuppa and led her up to the house.

We watched her skipping away, singing 'Tinkle, Tinkle, 'ickle dar' and then went over to the dragon-fruit tree. Its long cactus-like leaves trailed across the ground and you could hardly see the thick hairy trunk. It had been growing well and looked strong and healthy. Which was a relief, given that as far as we knew it was the only dragon-fruit tree that actually grew dragons. With the superhero squad's help over the last few months we'd been growing and releasing dragons galore. In fact we'd just had one of our biggest crops of dragon fruit so far.

There were signs everywhere of the little dragons, if you knew what you were looking for. The squashed empty dragon fruits and the mush and seeds mixed up with the soil, and then of course the telltale nibbled leaves and occasional bud-free bush.

'Good job your grandad doesn't mind his hard work being demolished,' Ted said, picking up a half-chewed cabbage. 'My dad gets cross if next door's cat so much as walks past his pansies.'

I laughed. 'A few chewed veggies is a small price to pay for growing dragons.'

Grandad didn't mind. Every time he saw a dragon pop out of one of the fruits his eyes twinkled with the

magic of it, every bit as
much as ours did. You
just never knew what
each new dragon would
be like. I thought of
the latest crop, the tiny
green-winged dragon
with its triple-tipped tail,

the amber one that shot luminous yellow flames as soon
as it hatched, and the pair of slender orange dragons,
covered in spikes, their curly horns glittering brightly.

All special. But none as amazing as Flicker, my
storm dragon, with his scales
that shimmered and shone.
I gazed up at the sky and
pictured myself riding up
there with my dragon.
Hollering to the stars.

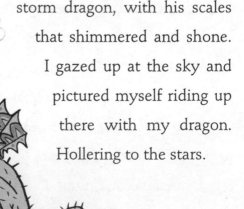

I was so distracted, remembering, I didn't look where I was treading. It was only when I felt something squish beneath my foot that I looked down. One of the branches of the dragon-fruit tree was trailing on the ground. And with a jolt of horror I saw that what my foot had landed on was the edge of a dragon fruit. A dragon fruit that had not burst, scattering seeds and mush and an excitable dragon. But a dragon fruit that still had something very much inside it.

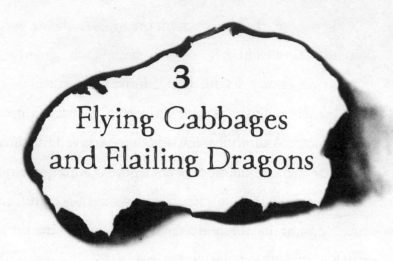

3
Flying Cabbages
and Flailing Dragons

I shrieked, giving Ted such a shock that he hurled the cabbage he'd been holding into the air. Quickly pulling my foot away, I peered down at the dragon fruit, terrified I'd stepped on the dragon inside and squashed it.

As Ted dodged the incoming cabbage and hurried over, I crouched down and gently lifted up the fruit, which had come away from the branch.

'What is it?' he cried. And then he saw what I was holding. 'You didn't . . . tread on that, did you?'

I nodded, my lips pinching back the squeak that was threatening to escape.

'Let's get it into the shed,' Ted said, trying very hard to sound calm.

'What if . . . ?' I said, still staring at the fruit.

Ted gave a little shake of his head. 'I'm sure it's fine.'

I carried it carefully towards the shed, Ted hustling in front, opening the door and clearing some space on the counter. I gently lay the fruit down and Ted pulled up the old stool for me to perch on. We watched it intently, time tick-tick-ticking past.

When the fruit was still not moving ten minutes later, we both started to fear the worst. I reached out and laid a hand on it, hoping I might feel the smallest movement that way.

'It feels jittery,' I said, turning to look at Ted, who was holding his breath. 'Like it's buzzing.'

Ted let out a gasp. 'That's good – at least there's something going on in there.'

You could never be sure just when a dragon would finally burst from their fruit. Having reassured ourselves that this one might just need more time,

I reached up to get Grandad's secret stash of Nana's jammy tarts. Ted looked as if he could do with one – or six, knowing him.

But as I pulled the tin off the shelf I dislodged a trowel. I watched in horror as it crashed onto the counter, landing right on top of the poor dragon fruit. I muttered a well-aimed insult at myself for being so clumsy.

Now, usually the dragons burst from the fruit on their own and flew off with very little help from us. But having almost squashed this one – not once but twice – I needed to be sure that it really was OK.

I looked around for something to break the skin of the fruit to help the little dragon on its way. Grabbing a pair of garden scissors, I leaned in close, holding the fruit with one hand.

'Do you think that's a good idea?' Ted said. 'I'm not saying you're clumsy . . . It's just –'

But before he could finish, the fruit burst open and the dragon shot out – straight into my face. The little dragon was so disorientated that he started flying in

crazy loops, banging into the light bulb, the shelves and every so often my head.

'Watch out!' Ted laughed, pulling me out of the way as the newly hatched dragon spun at me once more. He was moving incredibly fast, so I couldn't get a proper look at him. But I could see he had massive wings for the size of his body, which could have been why he was having so much trouble getting the hang of the whole flight thing.

'Open the door,' I cried, shielding my head with my arm.

Ted pushed the door and we stumbled out. Keeping low, we watched as the dragon zoomed back and forth before crashing headlong into one of Grandad's raspberry nets.

The more he flapped, the more tied up he became, till he'd wound himself into a tight cocoon, at which point he finally dropped to the ground.

'Poor little thing,' Ted giggled. 'He's certainly super-charged.'

I reached for the scissors on the counter and rushed over. Lifting the dragon up, I started cutting the net. His whole body was buzzing, and as the net loosened he started wriggling manically in my hands.

'Keep still,' I said frantically.

The dragon didn't listen. He just nipped my finger and scrabbled at my hands with his claws.

'Ow!' I yelped as he twisted and squirmed even more. 'Look I'm trying to help. But I can't if you won't let me.'

'Go slower,' Ted suggested.

I took a breath and waited for a lull in his frenzied wriggling.

As he settled down, I murmured, 'I'm just going to cut through the net. I can't rush in case I damage your wings. Please don't bite me. I'm not going to hurt you.'

Ted took a step back as if he wasn't sure the words would have much effect and didn't want to risk being bitten himself.

At last I managed to cut the net away and I lifted the hand I had laid gently over his back, expecting him to zoom off again. But for a second he sat there, wings held awkwardly.

Now he wasn't darting around above our heads

I could see the little dragon's body and wings more clearly. He was really pretty. Sky blue. The kind of crystal-blue sky you see on a bright winter's day. And there was a pattern of silver threads criss-crossing over his body and wings. His tail was narrow, a row of small spines running down it and ending in a glowing

silver zigzag. He stared back at me and I noticed then that his eyes were different colours. One was blue, the other white. The blue one sparkled like the sapphire on my mum's ring, while the white one looked like a swirling cloud.

And then he overbalanced and tumbled to the ground, just managing to flap his wings and take off before he hit earth.

'He seems to like you anyway,' Ted said as the dragon zigzagged through the air and headed haphazardly back towards me.

'In between bites,' I said. 'Maybe if I leave, he'll fly off.'

Ted's stomach rumbled loudly and he grinned apologetically.

'I could do with a bite myself. You're probably right. Let's hope so anyway or there won't be anything left of your grandad's garden!'

4
A Tricky
Sticky Situation

'Those runner beans been giving you the runaround?' Grandad said with a grin later, as I sat down to tea.

Lolli giggled and picked up two stray carrots she'd jettisoned from her plate and started racing them across the table.

'You look like you've crawled through a hedge,' Nana said. 'What on earth have you been doing out there?'

'Beans can be tricky to handle, isn't that right, Chipstick?' Grandad said.

'Especially when they're as fast as this one was,' I said between mouthfuls of casserole.

Grandad laughed and gave me a quick wink.

Nana gave us both a quizzical look and then shook her head, as if we were both as barmy as each other and welcome to it.

After second helpings of blackberry-and-apple crumble with custard, I headed upstairs.

We were staying at Nana and Grandad's for the weekend and as usual Lolli and I were sharing the room that looked over the garden. I didn't mind sharing – she'd inherited Grandad's ability to squirrel away treats, so there were always pockets of goodies hidden for us to discover.

I thought she'd taken it a bit far though when she squealed at me as I flopped onto my bed. Using my bed to hide things was not OK. I really didn't want to be covered in chocolate, jam or marshmallow.

'Lolli, can you not . . .' But she was already pulling me off the bed and peeling back the covers. I saw her shoulders sag and a little exclamation of horror escaped.

'What is it?' I asked, worried that my bed was going to be a mess of sticky goo.

'Herbert,' she whispered. 'You killded Herbert.'

Oh no! Who on earth was Herbert? Had she taken to hiding small animals in my bed now? I knew she was desperate for Mum to let her help look after the strays she brought home as part of her work as a vet. But she wouldn't have let Lolli bring one here. Would she?

I didn't want to look. What had I done? First almost squashing a dragon and now squidging a . . . a what? I peered closer, bracing myself for the worst. A splatted hamster? A flattened bunny? A crushed beetle?

And then I saw Herbert. He was none of these things. Herbert was a stick.

Not even a stick insect. Just a stick.

'Herbert in the hoppital,' Lolli said, pointing to a collection of sticks laid out on cotton-wool pillows next to her bed. 'I got to show Mummy what a good looker-afterer I am.'

'So you're practising your skills?'

She nodded eagerly.

'Well, it's a shame we can't tell her how well you looked after Tinkle. Then she'd know how good you are.'

Lolli smiled. Then she looked sadly at Herbert.

'Have you ever fixed a broken bone?' I asked, as I picked up and cradled a bent and sorrowful Herbert in my hands.

Lolli shook her head, tenderly holding his little twiggy arm.

'Right, well, no better time to learn,' I said. 'Run to the bathroom and get some sticky plasters.'

Lolli giggled, 'Sticky plasters for sticky Herbert.'

'Exactly,' I said. 'Now look lively – this could be tricky. A tricky sticky situation,' I added, grinning.

She gave a little frown and waggled her finger at me, before she hurried off, just in case I forgot the seriousness of the situation.

When she came back I realised I probably should have gone with her, you know, rather than staying with the stick.

She was draped in toilet roll and had stuck plasters all over her face. I guess to make them easier to carry, since her hands were full of Nana's face cream, antiseptic and toothpaste.

She seemed to find a use for it all as we fixed up not just Herbert, but the rest of her hospital inpatients: Bea, Malik, Sam and Elena, who were also all sticks – and the names of her friends at nursery. Finally we were just left with Stefan, which was our postman's name. Except this Stefan wasn't a postman – or a stick. He was a wooden spoon that Nana was all set to throw away due to the split down his 'head'. Lolli carefully wrapped a bandage round it and tucked him into a sock sleeping bag.

'Snug as a bug,' she said.

Sitting back on my bed, I had to admire her attention to detail.

'Night, night, Stefan.'

5
Off with the Dragons

I woke from a dream where I was flying, skimming low over a snaking glacier. Dragons of all sizes and colours flanked me, their scales glittering and their eyes fixed on a huge red sun melting into the horizon ahead. I threw off my covers, my ears still ringing with their bellows and roars, feeling ready for the world.

While Nana took Lolli on an expedition to get more toothpaste and toilet roll, Grandad and I headed down the garden.

'Seems like your zippy visitor had a right old party in my veggies,' Grandad said. 'And look at my pansies. Me and Jim are hoping to be picked to grow the flowers for the main display in the Village in Bloom show next year. And that dragon's just turned my flowers into confetti!'

'Sorry,' I replied. 'I really hoped he'd got used to his wings enough to fly off properly.'

'Oh well, never mind, Chipstick. I dare say we'll soon have things shipshape again.'

I looked at the mess and hoped the superhero squad were on their way. I didn't want Grandad to have to do much of the work. Although he was better since his stay in hospital, when they'd fixed his hip

and sorted out the right medicine for his poorly heart, I still kept one eye firmly on him. As if that could keep him safe. Every so often a picture of him lying in a hospital bed would pop into my head. And each time it was like an ice-cold wave had crashed over me, freezing my insides. I couldn't help thinking that if I took my eye off him, an icy wave might just sweep him away from me for good.

But there was no way he'd sit by and watch me do it all by myself.

Luckily it wasn't long before Kat, Kai, Ted and Liam arrived. As they came down the garden they caught sight of the state of the vegetable patch and I could see their collective shoulders sag. But being the superhero squad, they quickly got to work without a single moan.

'OK, captain, give us that spade and our orders,' Kai said to Grandad, taking the handle out of his grasp before he could object.

With so many extra hands, it wasn't long before we had set the garden to rights. Then, as Grandad headed back to the house for a sit-down, the rest of us made our way over to the dragon-fruit tree.

'Right,' Ted said. 'Dragon watch! I'm saying . . . purple tail, yellow body, black wings and two horns.'

'Breathing?' Liam asked.

'Green fire.'

There were a handful of fruits on the tree that were red and ripe. We gathered round one that was beginning to glow and bulge, grinning at each other.

Seconds later a tiny dragon burst out. It was a dull brown, with no horns and no spines.

'You were way off the mark,' Kai said.

It was hopping from foot to foot on the ground in front of us, shaking its wings to rid itself of the mess of pulp and seeds. When it turned, it suddenly noticed us all staring down at it. Alarmed, it lowered its head and spread out its wings. Fierce red eyes glared back at us. A pattern on the underside. And then its whole body shook and its scales lifted until they were all sticking out like tiny spears. We laughed and backed away.

'OK. OK,' Ted said, hands raised. 'We come in peace.'

We watched another hatch, this time a purple dragon with yellow wings and electric-blue spikes under its chin.

'It reminds me of Crystal,' Kat said. 'I wonder if this one breathes ice too.'

It didn't, but it did hiccup a breath of freezing fog that crystallised some onions.

When all the glowing fruits had hatched, we headed into the shed to raid Grandad's goodies tin.

'What happened in here?' Kat asked, noticing the wreckage the little clumsy dragon had caused bumping into things.

And so I told them about almost treading on the dragon fruit and the sky-blue and silver dragon that had shot out straight into my face.

'He really wasn't very good with those huge wings, and he was a bit hyper-charged,' Ted said.

'I think I might have launched at you, if you'd almost squashed me with your foot,' Liam replied.

'I bet you would.' Ted laughed, giving him a friendly nudge. We all remembered what Liam had been like before he joined the superhero squad. Though looking at him now, you'd be hard pressed to believe it. He grinned and shrugged, accepting the tease as fair comment.

'I didn't mean to,' I said defensively. 'I was just . . . distracted.'

Kat smiled. 'Off with the fairies – isn't that what your grandad says?'

'Off with the dragons in your case,' Kai laughed.

'We'll all be off with the dragons later, when we head to the nature reserve,' Ted said. 'I can't wait to see Sunny.'

'I was just thinking about Flicker, that's all, wondering how long he'll stay this time. Don't you think about that with Dodger?'

Kai shrugged. 'I guess.'

Kat snorted. 'Stop acting like you're any different to the rest of us,' she said. 'You're not the only one scanning the sky whenever they're not here, Tomas. You wouldn't believe the amount of times he's dragged me out of bed thinking he'd spotted them, only to find it was a cloud.'

6
Abominable Dragon Slobber

'Right, is everyone strapped in for take-off?' Grandad asked, giving a giggling Lolli a wink. We cupped our hands to our mouths and dragon-roared at the top of our voices. We were always ready to see the dragons!

He laughed. 'You know, actual dragons would be quieter than you lot!'

When we got to the nature reserve we all leaped out of the car.

'I'm popping over to collect some more seeds and pots. I'll pick you up on my way back,' Grandad said.

He bent down to give Lolli a hug. She wrapped

her arms around him and whispered something.

'I know you will, Lolli,' he said. He looked up. 'She's told me not to worry because she'll be keeping an eye on you.' He gave me a wink and I gave him a thumbs up. Lolli ran over and clung to my leg, as if to prove she was on the job.

Standing by the edge of the water, we peered across at the island. We could usually spot a glimmer

of scales or a tree that swayed oddly when there was no wind. But today there was no sign of them.

'They are still there, aren't they?' Kai asked.

There was a sudden whoosh of air that made my hair stick out. And I got that prickly feeling on the back of your neck when you have a sense you're being watched. I looked around, but couldn't see anything.

'Maybe they can see something we can't,' I said.

Then Dodger, whose camouflage skills were on a whole other level these days, suddenly appeared in front of us. We screamed and leaped back, Lolli squealing in excitement.

'Naughty,' she shrieked, wagging her finger at the dragon. He circled back and landed, thwacking his tail on the ground, obviously pleased with his surprise attack.

Lolli was jiggling about so much by this point I had to laugh. She wasn't allowed to sky-ride yet, so this was the only time she got to fly on a dragon, when we didn't go high, but skimmed the surface of the water. When I clambered up behind her, I could almost feel her body buzzing! It reminded me of the little dragon that had hatched the day before.

Once everyone was securely on Dodger's back, he tipped his head from side to side and stretched out his wings. And then he darted forward, leaving all our stomachs floundering in the mud.

On the other side of the water, the rest of the dragons were waiting. We jumped down and rushed over to them. Sunny immediately gave a rumble, sniffing out the treats Ted's pockets were always loaded with. Crystal blew an icy breath that frosted the trees around Kat, making icicle wind chimes for her to tap. Maxi, who often got a bit overexcited, blasted out a green breath that instantly made some ferns turn gigantic and swamped a laughing Liam. And Tinkle, the smallest of the dragons, tilted her head for Lolli to hug, filling the woodland with a song that made all our hearts soar.

And then there was Flicker. Too big now to sit on my shoulder and wrap his tail around my neck. I leaned against his flickering scales and he curled around me, his tail and head touching as he brought his kaleidoscope wing across to shelter me. Inside the little shimmering cocoon, I stared into his diamond eyes and breathed in the warm smoky smell of him.

As the yelling from the others got louder, I peeked out. Dodger, Sunny and Maxi were taking it in turns to suck up huge mouthfuls of water and then let them out

as steam. With a well-aimed breath from Crystal, the droplets were turning into glistening flakes of snow as they fell.

Lolli and Kat raced around with their tongues hanging out, until Kai told them they were basically eating frozen dragon slobber!

'Me and Ted are going to make an epic abominable snowman,' Liam cried. 'Come on, Ted – you're in charge of the body.'

Lolli had already grabbed my hand.

'Snow dragon, snow dragon . . .' she chanted happily.

Half an hour later, having finished our ice creations, we stopped to warm our hands and feet against the dragons.

I was pretty chuffed with our snow dragon. Lolli had found jet-black stones for its eyes and I'd used a stick to carefully carve scales along its sides. I'd curled the tail round and fashioned an arrowhead point just like Flicker's.

I looked over at Ted and Liam's round-bellied snowman. 'It's not very abominable, is it?' I said to Liam.

'No.' He laughed. 'Not very epic either.'

Suddenly a huge pile of snow hurtled at the snowman and sent it flying, covering Ted in the process. We all turned to see Dodger, one eye blinded by snow, flicking powdery drifts at us with his tail. It didn't take long for the other dragons to join in. They surrounded us, flinging snow till we looked pretty abominable ourselves. And then Flicker began making tiny whirling tornadoes that chased after us. Despite our best team effort to throw snowballs back, it was a bit one-sided.

'Hey.' I laughed. 'You should know by now that you can't beat a dragon in a snowball fight!'

'It wasn't me,' everyone cried in unison, laughing as the flurries of snow covered us, leaving us in a giggling heap.

Eventually we waved our hands in surrender and ran to the dragons, letting the warmth of them dry us through. After that we settled down to feast on the picnic supplies that Nana had packed for us.

'Can I adopt your nana, Tomas?' said Ted through a mouth full of cake. 'My gran is great, but right now she's too busy doing half-marathons to make me treats.'

'The amount my nana bakes, she could probably keep even Sunny satisfied,' I laughed.

'Challenge accepted!' Ted grinned.

It was Lolli who spotted Grandad on the other side of the lake, flashing his torch in our direction through the dusk.

'Tomas,' she said, pulling at my arm, 'Guppie here.'

She ran over to Tinkle and wrapped her arms around the dragon's neck. And got a long sonorous note in reply. A note that tugged at my heart.

I knew then, even without looking at Flicker, that the dragons were preparing to leave.

I watched everyone saying their goodbyes. Flicker nudged me with his nose and I looked up at him. I hated this part. I moved closer, wrapping my arms around his neck and squeezing my eyes shut. It never got any easier saying goodbye, because we never knew when we would next be seeing them.

As Dodger, Sunny, Maxi and Tinkle launched up into the air, Crystal blew an icy breath across the lake, freezing a bridge for us to cross that sparkled and shone and sent rainbows shooting out across the water.

She turned and Kat ran over to her, and for a moment their heads leaned together, Kat whispering something.

Flicker gave a rumble and blew a warm breath around me, and then he flapped his wings and lifted from the ground.

I stood with Kat and watched the dragons soar into the sky. As the others skated their way over the glittering bridge towards Grandad, I kept my own eyes fixed on the ruby glow disappearing from view.

7

Happy Flappy Floppy

When we got home after the weekend Mum and Dad were in what I'd call a happy-flappy state. All wide-eyed and talking really fast and waving their hands about. It turned out that while we'd been at Nana and Grandad's they'd had some pretty cool news. Mum had been asked to be resident vet at a local radio station. People could phone in and she'd give them advice on their poorly pets. And now Dad had had the brainwave of making little videos of Mum that they could put up on a website.

'I can record some of the animals and make a jingle. We'll have our own show,' he cried.

'Sounds great,' I said, laughing, as Mum caught Lolli up in a dance and began twirling her around the room.

'It'll be super-busy,' Mum called.

'You won't mind helping out, will you?' Dad said, swooping in and pulling me into the dance too.

'Do the dragon, do the dragon,' Lolli squealed.

And before I could reply, Dad had leaped onto the sofa, spread out his arms, thrown back his head and was roaring as loud as he could.

Now, it wasn't just hatching dragons I was looking after. I had something else hidden in my room that needed my care and attention. Quite a few somethings in fact. So leaving them to it, I headed upstairs.

I went straight over to my windowsill and peered down at the row of pots I'd lined up. Each one had a tiny seedling poking out. I groaned when I saw that four of the seedlings were lying limp and shrivelled. I tried lifting one up as I poured a little more water into the tiny pot, but as soon as I let go it flopped back down.

There was a small roar behind me and I turned to see Lolli in the doorway, in her best dragon pose.

'I'm an ice-cream dragon,' she giggled. Then seeing my sagging shoulders, she hurried over. 'I'm not a scary dragon,' she said apologetically.

I smiled. 'It's OK, Lolli, it's not you. It's these.' And I held up one of the seedlings. 'I just don't know what

I'm doing wrong,' I said sadly. 'All I know is I don't have Grandad's green fingers.'

'Are they sunflowers?' she asked, studying the little seedlings. 'I got a sunflower that grew this big.' And she flung her arm skywards and stood on tiptoe.

'No,' I said, and then, checking no one was out in the hall, I whispered, 'they're dragon-fruit trees.'

Lolli's eyes went wide and she clapped her hands.

I went on. 'Do you remember how Liam found a dragon-fruit tree at the botanic garden?'

She nodded and said seriously, 'Maxi breathed on all the fruit and all the little dragons grew.'

'That's right,' I said. 'Well, the thing is, that breath of Maxi's didn't just activate the fruit, it activated the seeds. Every time a dragon burst from a fruit, think of all those seeds being scattered.'

Her face screwed up and she stared at her fingers, obviously trying to do some important maths.

'Only seeds that have been breathed on by a special dragon like Maxi will ever become dragon-fruit trees that can grow dragons. So they're really important. That's a lot of little trees on the floor of that glasshouse, which might one day hatch dragons. We couldn't just leave them there. So we've been hunting for the seedlings, collecting them, and –'

She let out a squeak. 'You brunged them here?'

Now it was my turn to nod. 'The trouble is, dragon-fruit trees are really, *really* hard to grow.' I sighed.

Lolli looked from me to the windowsill. Gripping my arm, she inhaled deeply, closed her eyes and let out a long breath over the row of plant pots. 'Come on, little dragons, grow!' she whispered.

Lying in bed later, I felt as floppy as those seedlings. What if they all died under our care? Of course Maxi could breathe on more fruit and more seedlings might start to grow. But if we couldn't keep them alive, what then? Our dragon-fruit tree was the only one that grew dragons. That was a lot riding on our one plant. The whole future of the dragons, in fact.

One of the things I missed most about Flicker not living with me any more was night-times. Not having him tucked up next to me when I slept. When he dreamed happy dreams, his scales would shimmer, a kaleidoscope of turquoise, red, green and silver that coloured my own dreams and left me feeling like I'd just drunk a comforting mug of hot chocolate. I had loved hearing his contented rumble and feeling the warmth from his little body. I really needed that right now. When Dad did his rock-and-roll tuck-in that night, I lay there clutching Lolli's penguin heat pack,

Pengi. And tried to trick myself into believing Flicker was there beside me.

It didn't work though. I woke up sweating from a horrible dream where I was desperately digging through gardens full of petal confetti in search of Grandad, and sickly-looking seedlings cried at me and a giant-winged dragon had done an enormous poo all over our house.

I flung off the covers and looked down at Pengi. It wasn't his fault. Flicker was a hard act to follow.

8
Monday Apocalypse

I don't know about Monday mornings in your house, but in ours they can look a bit like we're starring in a disaster movie. People running in panic, half dressed, grabbing possessions. Like the world might end if I don't get to school on time or my sister doesn't have the right juice box – which, to be fair to my parents, given her capacity for supersonic meltdown, is probably a reasonable assumption.

But when I came down to breakfast, braced for the usual chaos, I was met by an eerie silence.

'Hello . . . ?' I called a little nervously, eyeing up

the half-eaten toast and contents of Lolli's bag spread across the table. A gerbil, chewing on one of her pencils, paused to look up at me as I made my way over to the back door.

I poked my head out and scanned the garden, where I spotted Mum, Dad and Lolli staring up at the roof.

It just shows what a hyperactive imagination I have that I felt quite so relieved to see them safe and unscathed. In the time it took to cross the kitchen, I'd played out at least six disaster-movie scenes in my head. The last one involving a giant wormhole opening up in our fridge.

'You all right, love?' Mum asked.

'Yeah,' I said, my voice sounding like I'd turned gerbil myself. 'What's going on? It's very . . . quiet for a Monday morning.'

'No telly,' Lolli said crossly, and she pointed up at the TV aerial, which was looking a bit bent and blacker than usual. I gave her a consoling squeeze. I knew how I felt when I couldn't watch my favourite TV programmes.

'I think we must have had some kind of power surge,' Dad said. 'Fried the electrics.'

'First the TV went bang, and then everything just stopped working,' Mum added, looking frazzled. On top of the usual Monday frenzy, Mum had her first appearance on the radio scheduled for that afternoon and the nerves were starting to show. She was wearing two different shoes and I also noticed that her clothes were covered in so much hair she looked more yeti than human.

'Don't worry, I'll have it sorted in time to listen,' Dad said chirpily. 'And I'll record it for you two,' he added, giving a disgruntled Lolli a wink. Lolli scowled even harder. She'd made it pretty clear that as Mum's veterinary nurse-in-training, she thought she should really be on the show too.

But when I got home from school later it was Dad who was looking frazzled.

Having brought back power to the house, he'd decided to make Mum a lemon drizzle cake to 'celebrate her celebrity'. He was usually a really tidy baker, but today the kitchen looked as if a troop of chimpanzees had thrown a tea party. And by thrown, I mean actually thrown. Everything was covered in a white layer of flour. The six excitable mice that had got loose and the shrieking parakeet probably weren't helping to calm things down.

'I only popped out to make a quick call,' Dad said.

'I think the animals decided to "help".'

Thankfully Mum's part in the show had gone really well, so she didn't even notice the cake-splattered kitchen.

There was a knock on the back door and Ted's face appeared, his eyes lighting up when he saw Dad preparing to take the lemon drizzle cake out of the oven. Honestly I think he can smell cake the way sharks smell blood, from miles away.

When we got to my room, I groaned. The door had been left open and some of the animals had clearly decided wrecking the kitchen was just not enough.

'Yikes,' said Ted. 'It looks like you had a tornado over for tea.'

I stared at the books, Lego and pots of pencils that lay scattered across the floor, and my box of comics, which had been completely shredded.

'I think you might need a new wing,' Ted said, holding up a chewed piece of cardboard. I took it from him and sighed. Our teacher Miss Jelinski had set us all a challenge to make a costume as part of our Myths and Legends topic. And of course I'd chosen a dragon. At least the box I was using as a body was still intact. As I started tidying up, Ted wrinkled his nose and grimaced.

'Something stinks,' he said.

He was right.

'Oh no,' I said, wondering which of the animals had done the smelly deed. 'Can you help me find it?'

Ted didn't look overly enthusiastic.

'Come on, we've dealt with worse,' I said. 'At least it won't explode over us.'

'Um . . . I wouldn't be too sure of that,' Ted said.

'What do you mean?'

He pointed to my bed and I suddenly saw what he'd seen. There was something just visible under my bed. Something half covered by a comic. Something bright blue. And scaly.

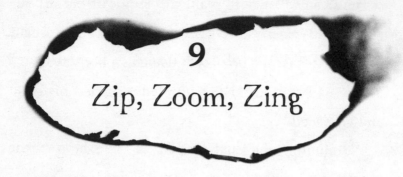

9
Zip, Zoom, Zing

Gently I lifted the comic. There, curled up and fast asleep, was the little sky-blue dragon, his huge wings folded back and the silver threads along his body only faintly visible now.

The dragon's eyes blinked open and, seeing us standing there, he immediately launched himself out from under the bed. With a whoosh he shot past me, making the hair on the back of my head stick out.

'Looks as if I was right about him liking you,' Ted said with a grin, as the dragon began circling above me.

Suddenly the wrecked kitchen and the state of my bedroom made a lot more sense. And so did that feeling I'd had by the lake of being watched. I remembered the way my hair had stuck out then too, after a similar whoosh of air.

'I think we've just found out who started the snowball fight!' I said. 'He must have followed me.'

Just then the door opened and Lolli skipped in waving her hands – which had socks on. Her new thing was making sock puppets, and these two had large yellow and pink pompoms glued to their foreheads – and they both seemed to have about five eyes.

She froze when she saw the dragon. I raced across the room, quickly checking the hallway and closing the door behind her.

'Shhhh,' I urged, jamming my finger to my lips.

Lolli, after a second of holding her breath in utter excitement, clasped her hand over her mouth to stop herself squealing and then started dancing round the room to jiggle it out instead.

'Lolli,' I hissed. 'Calm down.'

But there was no containing the little whirlwind that is my sister. And all the uncontrollable jiggling had a similar jiggling effect on the dragon who bashed his way around the room.

Lolli clapped her hands in delight and chased around after him, sock-puppet mouths opening and closing in excitement.

The dragon sped up even more. I could see the silver threads on his wings growing brighter, spreading down his body.

'Watch out,' Ted cried, ducking out of the way of the dragon's flight path.

I turned back just in time to see him fly up to my lampshade, where his tail flicked against the bulb. For a second there was a brilliant flare of light and then it burst, scattering tiny fragments of glass.

Ted picked up Lolli and swung her onto my bed out of harm's way.

'Zing, zing,' she giggled as the dragon, startled by the shattering sound, zoomed over our heads.

I grabbed a handful of ash from the tin on my desk and held it out, hoping that this little whirlwind of a dragon might be drawn to it as the others had been. But either he was too revved up to notice it or he just wasn't interested.

'What are we going to do?' I cried.

'Follow your advice,' Ted said. 'Let's all get on

your bed. If we sit quietly, maybe he'll calm down.'

He finally settled on an empty shelf and peered down at the three of us, sitting cross-legged on my bed.

'Now what?' I whispered.

Ted shrugged.

'Perhaps if I open the window, he'll fly out,' I suggested.

I slid off the bed and very slowly edged my way towards the window. The dragon tilted his head to watch me. I pushed the window as wide as it would go and looked hopefully at him. He didn't move.

'Maybe Zing's hungry,' Lolli whispered.

'Zing?' I asked.

'He's all zingy,' she said happily.

Having calmed down now, she too slid off the bed and tippy-toed her way towards the door.

'Can you go with her?' I asked Ted. 'I'd better stay with him.'

'With Zing,' Lolli said sternly.

'It looks like someone's got a name,' said Ted.

I smiled. Then, keeping one eye firmly on the dragon so he didn't dart through the door after them, I nodded at Lolli.

'Right – with Zing,' I said.

While they were gone, Zing and I watched each other. Every so often the little silver point on his tail would flash. And he would scratch his claws along the plastic shelf. But at least he stayed where he was.

Just as I was deciding I should go and look for Ted and Lolli, the door opened and they came in, arms full of food. Though I also noticed Ted was licking his lips.

'We didn't know what to bring,' Ted said.

'So we brunged Zing a bit of everything,' Lolli said proudly.

First off I decided to offer him some broccoli, Flicker's favourite. He fluttered down and stared at the green vegetable. To be honest he looked about as impressed as I do when Mum puts broccoli on my plate.

So next I served up one of Flicker's favourite treats, salt-and-vinegar crisps. He took a sniff and bashed the packet with his tail, smashing the contents to smithereens.

After that we tried: cheese, a biscuit, an apple, bread, one of Grandad's caramel toffees, a pot of yoghurt, a kipper, a jam tart, a ham sandwich and a piece of Dad's liquorice. He wasn't keen on any of these. And he proceeded to swipe his tail at each offering. He perked up when Lolli offered him the soggy remains of a squeezed-out lemon from the lemon drizzle cake. But in the end he was far more interested in my remote-control car and Lolli's talking Batman.

I peeled a kipper, which had been flung like a Frisbee by the dragon's tail, off the wall. I wasn't sure how I was going to explain to Mum the bizarre picnic lunch laid out in my room. I didn't think she'd believe we'd really craved jam kippers.

'Let's give it a rest,' I said. 'He can't be that hungry. Maybe I should try shooing him towards the window.'

'I dunno,' Ted said doubtfully. 'It's wide open and he hasn't flown out.'

At this Zing flew down from my desk and hopped his way under my bed, back where we'd found him earlier. We knelt down and peered in at him.

'He's got half my wardrobe under there,' I said, pointing to the pile of jumpers and the bobble hat.

'And most of your socks, by the looks of it,' Ted laughed.

Lolli grinned. 'He builded a nest.' And we watched as Zing wriggled down into the comfy hollow and started wrestling my clothes into some sort of order around him.

'Definitely looks like he's made a home for himself,' Ted agreed. 'Look, if he doesn't want to go,

you might upset him by trying to boot him out. And I'm not sure your room could take that!'

'You're not saying I should let him stay?'

'Maybe, just for a bit. Until he's ready to leave. I'm sure he'll head off soon enough. You should make the most of it while he's here.'

Given the devastation Zing had already caused, I wasn't sure this was a good idea. Who knew what he'd get up to while I was sleeping, when I couldn't keep an eye on him? But in the end I decided Ted might be right about not upsetting him by trying to shoo him outside. Zing had curled up in his nest under my bed and seemed peaceful enough for now, but I left the window wide open, as an escape route, in case it turned out he didn't want to stay after all.

10
Dragon 1,
Solar System 0

The next day I woke up roasting hot. I'd gone to sleep under my quilt, with an extra blanket and tucked up with a toasty Pengi. All to shield myself against the cold air from the window I'd left open. I leaned over the edge of the bed and peered underneath. There was no sign of Zing.

And then something wriggled against my feet and I realised why I was quite so toasty. There, curled up on the very end of my bed, was the little blue dragon. He lifted his head and stared at me, his sapphire eye sparkling, his white eye a swirling cloud. Feeling the

warmth of him against my feet reminded me again how much I missed having Flicker tucked up next to me.

'Up-getting time, Tomas,' Dad called loudly from the other side of the door, borrowing the phrase Lolli used to say when she was smaller.

Zing twisted round and I yelped as his tail zapped my toe with its pointy end. Flicker had never done that!

The next minute, a deafening blast of music blared out from the room below. It was quickly turned down as Dad reset the volume, but had been alarming enough to startle Zing into a panic. He immediately launched up into the air on a collision course with my solar-system mobile. Earth spun out of orbit and careered into the black hole behind my desk. And then the sun exploded as Zing's tail sent it flying. Goodbye, solar system!

As I got dressed I kept one eye on Zing.

'I'm going to school,' I declared.

Zing, who had been taking a keen interest in my radio alarm clock, flapped up and started circling my head.

'I'm going to leave the window open,' I said. 'For you,' I added to make things clear.

Zing fluttered over to the windowsill and bobbed his head as he stared out at the garden. But he didn't fly off.

I walked over to the door, pulled it open and stepped out into the hall. Looking back, I whispered, 'Please don't wreck my room while I'm out.'

As I walked out through the gates after school I wondered if I would go home to utter devastation, my room a shredded claw-scratched disaster zone. Or maybe I wouldn't even have a home. I hadn't seen Zing breathe fire yet, but Flicker had taken his time to start emitting the blue flames he was capable of. Who knew what Zing would one day unleash. As I pictured the smouldering remains of my house, I started running.

I let out a ragged sigh and slowed down as I came round the corner. The house was at least still standing and there were no firemen lining the pavement or smoke billowing from my bedroom window.

Upstairs, I actually found everything just as I'd left it. And no sign of Zing. Not even under my bed. Surprising me, my stomach did a little half-flutter of disappointment as I made my way to the open window and stared out.

It seemed Zing had left after all.

As I turned my gaze away from the sky and back to the windowsill in front of me, I saw that Zing had left some pretty deep scratches in it. I moved a couple of the seedlings further along to hide them, and noticed that another one of them had fallen and was lying limply on the soil in the pot.

The first few times I'd visited the botanic garden with the superhero squad we'd found lots of the tiny dragon-fruit shoots, but recently we'd come back with just one or two. I began picturing lone seedlings being unwittingly trampled on.

With Zing gone and the rest of the superhero squad busy for the afternoon, I decided it was time for another trip.

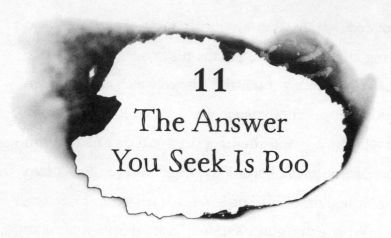

11
The Answer
You Seek Is Poo

When I got to the entrance of the botanic garden, I showed my pass to the girl in the little hut. Not that she even noticed. She had her head in a book called *Stories of Botanical Exploration* and was chewing intently on the end of a pencil.

I made my way along the path, past the ornamental pond with its stepping stones and towards the lawn with the big glasshouses.

The dragon-fruit tree was right at the other end, and the quickest way to get to it was by walking straight down the corridor, past the vines and colourful orchids that grew along the walls. But you could also enter the hot and steamy rainforest room and walk through there to reach the slightly cooler area where the dragon-fruit tree grew.

I always went the long way. Wandering through there made me feel like Elvi and Arturo venturing into the rainforest. They were the ones who'd found the Hidden Dragon City in Mexico and discovered the last two active dragon-fruit seeds in an ancient temple, hidden in the jungle. Elvi had lived in Nana and Grandad's house before them and Arturo had given Elvi one of the seeds to take back with her, so that there would be hope in two places, he said. The seed he kept never grew, but Elvi's did. And she had cared for it in her garden – and for the dragons.

And now here I was, searching for more seeds.

Machete in hand – well, the bit of branch I'd picked up on the way in – I set off, keeping my eyes peeled for scorpions and snakes and jungle jaguars. Soon I'd spotted five new species of insect, tracked an ocelot, narrowly avoided being eaten by a python and followed a troop of spider monkeys.

Just as I took a step forward to peer through some giant leaves, something rocketed down in front of me. I jumped back, imagining some bat had decided to start dive-bombing me. But then I caught a flash of bright blue and silver. I spun round in time to see the threads flaring along Zing's back.

'Hey!' I said, grinning. 'I thought I'd lost you there. Where did you disappear to? And how did you even get in here?'

I looked around but couldn't see any windows left ajar.

Zing flew down, circled me and then zipped out of sight behind a bush.

I laughed. 'I guess I'm not the only one who's been tracking things. You know, you'd be an amazing spy. I had no idea you were following me.'

He fluttered down and did a little somersault in front of me, and I could almost feel the air crackling

around him, like static. He seemed to be enjoying his
game of stealth and surprise as much as I was.

'Come on then,' I whispered. 'Time to get serious.'
Dropping my machete, I braced myself for the harder
task of looking for more seedlings.

'Let's see just how good your tracking skills are,
shall we?' I said, leading him towards the cooler part of
the greenhouse where the dragon-fruit tree grew.

He tilted his head and looked at me quizzically.
Hopefully if he saw me find one of the seedlings,
he'd cotton on and sniff some more out, like giving
something to a tracker dog.

But as I continued on, scanning the ground, I found nothing. And either Zing wasn't getting the idea or he wasn't having any luck either.

Checking no one was nearby, I stepped off the path and headed deeper into the undergrowth, crawling on all fours through the densest parts.

I couldn't see Zing now, but I hoped he still had an eye on me. I was about to call it a day when I finally spotted one lone seedling peeping out of the dirt. It looked like it was healthy and I wondered if I should just leave it there rather than uprooting it. I could always mark where it was and keep watch over it. But then a khaki boot landed two inches from my hand, almost squashing the seedling.

'What are you doing, may I ask?' came a voice.

I looked up and saw a woman peering down at me over the rim of her glasses, not looking terribly pleased.

'I know I have terrible eyesight, but I'm pretty sure you're not one of my exotic specimens.'

I slowly stood up, keeping my feet either side of the seedling to protect it, wondering exactly how much trouble I was going to be in and hoping more than anything that Zing would stay hidden.

'Visitors are expected to stay on the paths,' she said.

'Yes, I'm really sorry, I got a little lost,' I stuttered.

She looked me up and down and said, 'Explorer, are you?'

It was the kind of thing someone might say as a joke, but there was no smile or raised eyebrow so I wasn't sure how to take it.

Then a butterfly flew past and her face suddenly lit up. She watched it land on a nearby leaf. As she studied it she kept making little contented humming noises. She was totally absorbed by it, and, remembering how close her boot had come to squashing the tiny fledgling dragon-fruit tree, I quickly decided it might be safer with me after all and took the opportunity to grab a pot from my pocket and scoop the little seedling into it.

'Did you know,' she said, turning back to me, 'there is a butterfly in the rainforests of New Guinea that has a wingspan that is more than twenty centimetres across. Largest in the world. And the Atlas moth, the white witch moth and the Hercules moth have wingspans of up to thirty centimetres.'

I didn't know, but I did think she'd probably get on well with Ted, who also has a head full of these sorts of facts.

'Wow!' I said. And then deciding to be brave, I added tentatively: 'Do you think I could ask you a few questions?'

'School project?' she asked. 'Rainforest topic?'

I nodded. 'Doing some research,' I replied, not wanting to fib outright.

'Well, I've been studying botany for nearly twenty-five years,' she said. 'I've worked here since I was a student. I always have time for a fellow researcher.'

She extended a hand.

'Chouko,' she said. 'Chouko Sato. And you are?'

'Tomas Liffy.'

'Delighted to meet you,' Chouko said, smiling.

My eyes flicked to the dense undergrowth and Chouko followed my gaze, obviously curious. I quickly looked away and smiled, hoping Zing would keep well out of sight.

'So you know all about the things that grow in the rainforest?' I asked.

She gave a little laugh. 'I take it you know how big

an area rainforests cover? And what a wealth of flora and fauna they contain? Even after all these years, I only know some things. But I will try my best to help.'

'I've been trying to grow something, you see, some seedlings. But they keep dying. I just want to know what I'm doing wrong.'

'It's difficult to answer that without knowing exactly what you are growing. Plants can be very fussy. What is it that you have?'

'A . . . a . . . cactus,' I said, hoping that would be enough.

She nodded.

'Well, cacti like a well-drained soil. How often are you watering your little friends?'

'I'm not overwatering,' I said quickly, remembering how Grandad and I had read in Elvi's book about the dangers of this.

'That's good. But do your containers have holes in the bottom just in case?'

I shook my head.

'Cacti really do not like to get their feet wet. I would suggest making some small holes in the bottom. Also, use a mister, not a watering can. And finally, get yourself some earthworm castings. Very natural fertiliser.' She chuckled and added, 'Worm poo.'

12
A Flicker of a Dream

Once I'd thanked Chouko and said goodbye, I spent a few minutes loitering by the glasshouses. After that final glimpse I'd caught of Zing heading into the trees, he'd disappeared again. Now I didn't know whether to wait for him or make my way home. How responsible was I for this little dragon?

I took a tentative step towards the gate, and suddenly he zipped out from a bush, his tail flashing silver.

I grinned. 'I can't help feeling you're playing a bit of a game with me.' He swished his tail and did three somersaults in a row. Yup, definitely playing a game.

The first thing I did when I got home, after opening the window for Zing, was poke holes in the bottom of the pots containing the seedlings. Despite being careful about not overwatering I found a couple of them did have wet feet, so I carefully lifted out their straggly roots and repotted them. I also decided to ask Grandad about getting some worm poo. He could add it to his order of ladybirds, the little army of bug helpers who protected his garden from an invasion of pests.

The next thing I did was pull out my dragon costume. It was now only a few days until the dress-up day at school and I had loads more to do on it. Apart from still needing to make the head, quite a few of the scales along the body had already peeled off and needed repairing, and thanks to Zing I was one wing short. I wanted to look epic. A majestic dragon. And

I was definitely going to put the time in to make that happen.

By the time Lolli came in to declare – with her kazoo – that it was teatime, I had cramp in both legs and aching arms from sitting cross-legged, sticking on all the scales I had painstakingly coloured in.

'Ooh, pretty,' Lolli said, her eyes wide.

That was the reaction I was going for.

'Thanks, Lollibob.' I grinned. 'Should make quite an entrance.'

After tea I came back to my room to find Zing wrestling one of my jumpers. He'd wriggled inside and got all tangled up. I unhooked him and he hopped out, one of my socks clutched in his claws. I watched as he disappeared under my bed into the nest he'd made, which I noticed had grown a lot bigger. It certainly looked like he was making himself at home.

I dug out my old dressing gown that had a black mark from where Flicker had scorched it, and pushed it towards Zing.

'Maybe you can use this instead,' I whispered. 'Otherwise I might not have any clothes left to wear.'

When I crawled into bed later I could hear him scratching away and my thoughts returned to Flicker. I pictured my shimmering friend and the times we'd spent together when he was small. The way he had settled on my shoulder, his tail curling round my neck, his warm breath tickling my ear. His scales that shone, flickering through every colour. His endless sneezes, shooting out sparks I had to race to snuff out. The quiet rumble as he slept, tucked in beside me. And the dreams we shared.

On so many nights, I had flown over the forest with the Hidden City below us, feeling the fiery heat in my belly as I roared out a brilliant burst of blue flame. I had soared above a volcano, a blaze of dragons erupting from its crater, colours illuminating the sky. And then I had swooped and dived and finally landed to greet them.

As I wriggled down under the covers, I conjured Flicker in my mind, screwing my eyes tight shut so no detail would escape.

If I couldn't keep him here, I would keep him in my dreams.

13
Dragon on the Loose

The next day as I came bundling in through the school gates I saw the rest of the superhero squad huddled together, whispering urgently. I rushed over to them.

'What's going on?' I asked.

Liam turned and hissed, 'We just heard a group of Year Three girls giggling about the dragon in the hall.'

'What if one of them has got lost and found its way into school?' said Kai.

'We can't have a rerun of the time our lot got into Mrs Battenberg's canteen,' Kat said. 'That was mayhem.'

I glanced at Ted, who was looking as worried as I felt. He was probably wondering if his advice to let Zing stay might be about to come back and bite him in the bum.

But there wasn't time now to tell everyone about Zing. We needed to act – and fast. Once Zing started careering around with those massive wings, he'd be hard to miss.

'Come on,' I cried. 'We need to catch him before anyone else sees him.'

We raced through the double doors into the hall and stopped. Seeing the kids all crowding around something, my heart sank. I looked at Ted and Liam, red-faced from running. Their wide eyes said it all. This was bad.

'What do we do?' Kai hissed.

'We could wait for him to do a poo,' Ted said. 'That's sure to clear the hall, once it explodes everywhere. Or maybe he'll come if he smells ash. Has anyone got any on them?'

'You keep calling it a "he",' Liam said, ignoring Ted's question and looking thoughtful. 'We don't know it's a he.'

Given I was pretty sure the dragon was Zing, I was about to say that I did know, and I'd explain why later. But then I stopped. Actually Liam was right, I didn't know. I'd just assumed Zing was a he, right from the start. Like I had with Flicker. Maybe neither of them were boys. Anyway, I didn't have time to dwell on that now. I just had to catch him . . . or her.

'One of the teachers might come in any minute,' Kai said in alarm.

'Then we need to be quick,' I replied. 'I'll grab the dragon, if you can handle this lot.'

They nodded and, leading the way, I ran headlong into the scrum.

I barrelled my way through the complaining wall of people, elbows jabbing me left, right and centre, and tumbled onward. I just had to dive on Zing, scoop him up and get out of there before the army of elbows could come for me.

I saw a flash of what might be his silver tail. Pushing past the last few onlookers, I launched myself forward. That exact same moment, Kat shrieked, 'Tomas! No!'

Too late. I couldn't stop the force of my momentum now.

Nothing clears a hall like a scream and blood. And I did scream, and there was a torrent of blood. Faces do not enjoy meeting floors at speed, I can tell you. As I lay there, blood from my nose streaming down my face, I saw Kat go up and introduce herself to the dragon.

The dragon who was, in fact, not a dragon. But a girl in a costume – wearing a detachable dragon head, cardboard wings and a bright grin.

She reached down to pull me up, keeping a grip on her home-made dragon head with the other.

'You might think I'd be the one hoping to fly, given I've actually got some wings,' she said with a grin.

She stretched out her arms to show the wings off properly. They were sculpted from cereal boxes, cut into feathery shapes and tied together with string.

They moved like layered feathers and the effect was *really* cool. Of course dragons don't actually have feathery wings, but no one could deny the work that had gone into them. I thought of the peeling scales on my dragon costume, hastily scribbled in felt-tip pen. They didn't look half as good as these.

'But it's not dress-up day today,' I said.

'I know that now!' She laughed. 'No one told me they'd moved it,' she added with a shrug. 'Never mind, it's good to make an entrance on your first day. At least everyone will know who I am.'

'Er . . . yeah,' I mumbled, still holding my nose, no longer sure if I was wincing from the pain or from the fact I'd just seen how incredibly intricate and detailed her dragon's head was.

'So you've met Tomas,' Kat said cheerily. 'And that's Ted, Liam and my brother Kai.' The girl waved at them each in turn and they grinned and put up a hand in greeting.

'That is an awesome costume,' Liam said.

'It's amazing,' Kai agreed.

Ted gave me a sideways look. I hadn't told anyone apart from him I was planning to make a dragon costume. You know that expression 'to steal someone's thunder'? It means to spectacularly upstage someone. Jumping in and doing something just before they do, and so destroying the effect they'd worked so hard to create. Well, she had just stolen all my thunder and most of my lightning too.

'I'm Aura,' the girl said, raising her dragon head like she was tipping a hat. 'I'm new.'

Just then a couple of the more snooty Year Five girls approached and started sniggering when they saw Aura's costume.

Without even thinking, the superhero squad closed ranks around her. Hastily shaking off the mental image of me standing forlorn in my dragon costume looking embarrassed and ignored, I quickly stepped forward to join them.

We glared at the girls, until they tutted, rolled their eyes and sauntered off, arms linked like they were one mean articulated animal.

'Don't mind them,' Kat said.

Suddenly a booming voice descended on us.

'Could I interest you in a bit of education? If you're not too busy larking around in here, that is.'

We all turned to see the scowling face of our teacher Mr Firth.

'Sir, this is Aura, she's new,' Kat said.

'Yes,' said Mr Firth. 'New and already causing disruption, I see. Get to class now, the lot of you.'

As we hurried out of the hall, Aura whispered, 'Guess he's not a fan of dragons then?'

I shook my head, remembering the devastation caused by the dragons on our last class trip: the burning barn, the rocket-propelled bull and the ice-skating ostrich, not to mention the flying piglets.

'No, he really isn't,' I said with a grin.

14
Cows Go Moo, Dads Go Quack

I think Aura had been hoping to show the rest of the class her dragon costume. Mr Firth, though, was having none of it. Nothing was going to distract him from the spelling test he was giving us.

'I know it's the wrong day, but you'd think he'd be a bit interested,' Aura said sadly.

'It's Miss Jelinski who set the costume homework,' Kai said. 'She'll be back on Friday and she'll love to see it. We only have Mr Firth for two days a week.'

'Thank goodness,' Liam said, and we all gave a collective shudder at the thought of a whole week with Mr Firth. We'd all hoped we'd have smiley Mr Peters joining Miss Jelinski in our last year of primary, not frowning Mr Firth.

'I'm going to miss . . .' Kat said, but then stopped. I saw Kai give her a funny look and she added, 'Er . . . yeah, Miss will love it.'

Thanks to Mr Firth keeping us late at lunchtime to work on more spellings, I didn't get a chance to tell the rest of the superhero squad about Zing. But I did manage to pass a secret note around, asking if they could come to mine after school.

When I got home I found Dad quacking at the sofa. These days very little surprises me, but this was a bit weird, even for Dad. He was wearing his big headphones and leaning over the back of the sofa, one hand stretched out, holding what looked like a large mouse on a stick. I realised the mouse was actually one of those big fluffy microphones, at exactly the same moment I recognised that he was quacking the Superman theme tune.

'All right, Dad?' I said. 'How's the radio jingle for Mum's show coming on?'

He looked up and grinned. 'You know, it's harder than you'd think to record animal noises. For a start, the rabbits, hamster and corn snake your mum's looking after at the moment, don't say much at all. I'm hoping I'll have better luck with Daisy.'

'The duck behind the sofa?' I said.

'What? No, Daisy's a bearded lizard. I'm just not sure what sound they make.'

I opened my mouth to reply and realised I didn't know what to say to that, so left him to it.

I popped into the kitchen to grab a snack. Everywhere I looked there was more evidence of Dad's failed attempts to talk to the animals. He was definitely no Doctor Dolittle. Still, at least it meant any other unexplained mess was unlikely to be noticed!

I couldn't help groaning when I went upstairs though and saw the state of my room. Added to the mess Zing had made and which I still had to clear up, Mum's animal house guests had obviously got in there too. Maybe trying to escape Dad and his hairy microphone. Luckily the little pots of seedlings on the windowsill seemed to have been spared.

I sank onto my bed. I evidently needed locks and bolts on my bedroom door to keep all the wildlife at bay. I started picturing great iron bars like castles have – at which point I got a bit carried away and imagined myself a moat and drawbridge too.

The next second the door burst open and Ted,

Liam, Kat and Kai came barrelling in. So much for my castle defences!

'I think your dad has gone officially doolally,' Ted said. 'We passed him crawling on the floor, smacking his lips like a goldfish.'

'He doesn't know what a bearded lizard sounds like,' I said, suddenly too weary to explain any further. Weirdly that seemed to satisfy Ted.

Liam moved a heap of Lego bricks out the way and sat down on the chair by my desk. The heap had been a Star Wars land cruiser that had taken me weeks to make.

'You're dead lucky,' Liam said. 'My mum would never let me have my room in this state. She's on at me to tidy up if I leave a sock on the floor.'

'We always thought it was Flicker making a mess,' Kai said with a laugh, 'but maybe you were just using dragons as a cover for your natural slobbiness.'

I looked at Ted, who grinned and said, 'I reckon it's time you spilled the beans about your little visitor.'

15
Seedlings and Superheroes

'You remember the little dragon I told you about?' I said.

'The one you trod on?' Kai asked.

'I didn't actually tread on him,' I said quickly. 'But yes, him. Well, he didn't exactly fly away after that.'

I knelt down and pointed under the bed, showing them the nest of clothes.

'He just kept turning up,' I said.

'So where is he now?' Kat asked, peering into the nest.

'That's the thing,' I said. 'I don't know. He's not like

Flicker. He just appears, and then he'll disappear again.'

'And when he is here,' Ted said, 'he can be a bit super-charged. Isn't that right, Tomas?'

I nodded and laughed. 'He's certainly a live wire. And he doesn't seem that interested in ash either, which isn't helping matters.'

Kat got up and peered out of the window. 'I hope he comes back. I'd like to see him before . . .' She suddenly stopped talking and gave a little cough. 'Before he . . . you know, goes north.'

I noticed Kai giving her a weird look that involved some eyebrow wiggling. There had been a lot of these 'looks' between the twins recently.

Before I could quiz either of them, Kat lifted up one of the pots from the windowsill. 'So, how are the seedlings doing?' she asked.

I went over and took the pot from her.

'I don't know what I'm doing wrong,' I said, 'but they just keep dying. I managed to find another one yesterday, but it took ages and I didn't see any more

while I was looking. These could be all that's left.'

I told them about meeting Chouko and the advice she'd given.

'I don't know if it'll work,' I said. 'But I'm ready to try anything. Of course, she might have been able to tell me more if I hadn't just said it was a cactus.'

'You were only trying to protect the tree from anyone getting too nosy,' Kai said.

'You can't blame yourself,' Kat said gently. 'None of us have come up with a solution. You're doing your best. And you're not the only one to have had problems growing a dragon-fruit tree. We know how difficult it is. I mean Arturo never managed to get his seed to grow, did he?'

'No, but Elvi did,' Ted piped up. 'Maybe she can help. Why don't we look at her notebooks again, in case we missed something.'

Through Elvi's diary and notebooks, which we'd found hidden away under Grandad's shed, we'd already learned some important things, like the fact that dragons and dragon-fruit trees love ash. We'd also learned that not only had Arturo never managed to grow a tree, more alarmingly, we had discovered that one day Arturo had walked into the Mexican forest and never returned. Ever since I'd heard that, I had always wondered what had happened to him.

I couldn't help hoping that perhaps he'd found something in the forest. Another tree maybe. And that he had stayed to protect it. And possibly to protect the dragons that grew on it. But maybe that was all just wishful thinking. He could have died in the forest for all we knew.

Whatever had happened to him though, we were now facing the same struggles he had. And I wished we could find out more about what he'd learned, so we could avoid making the same mistakes. Maybe Ted was right and there were things we had missed. From Elvi – and maybe even from Arturo.

'I vote we spend tomorrow digging,' Kat said.

We all looked at her sceptically.

'Digging for information,' she explained. She smiled at me. 'My bet is, there is a whole lot more Elvi and Arturo can tell us. And I want to find out what that is.'

You know sometimes it can feel like best friends actually read your mind. The superhero squad were always doing that. I grinned back and nodded eagerly.

That night my dreams flickered, vivid and bright. I was standing in the forest where Elvi and Arturo had ventured. The air thrummed with the buzz of insects, the wild song of exotic birds and the loud calls of howler monkeys.

Out of the corner of my eye I saw something move. I spun round and caught the glinting scales of a tail disappearing into the greenery. I stumbled after it, but the trees plucked at my sleeves and stuck out their roots, tripping me so I landed in the litter of leaves. I scrabbled to my feet and searched again, desperate now. But the gleam of dragon scales had vanished.

16
Cake-Fuelled Discovery

The next day after school, we all met at Nana and Grandad's. At the news the superhero squad were coming, Nana had gone into baking overdrive. There were multiple plates of jam tarts, a whole Victoria sponge cake, tiny salted caramel muffins, sugary shortbread triangles, gooey chocolate brownies and even some peppermint fondant sweets.

Ted went dreamy-eyed when he walked into the kitchen and saw everything spread out across the table.

'Yup, definitely adopting your nan,' he said.

Everyone loaded their plates and, thanking Nana, headed upstairs.

'You're the best,' I said, giving her the squeeziest squeeze.

Kat was waiting for me at the bottom of the stairs. 'So where's Zing?' she asked.

I shrugged. 'I don't know,' I said. 'I expect he'll turn up though. And there's plenty of time. We can look for him in the garden later if you like.'

She looked a bit disappointed. 'Come on,' I said. 'Or Ted will eat that whole extra plate of muffins he took up!'

Joining the others in the room I shared with Lolli, we started unloading boxes, pulling out Elvi's diary and the heaps of notebooks. We hadn't managed to read even half of it since I'd found it all hidden under Grandad's shed – mainly because of Elvi's handwriting, which was tiny and almost indecipherable in places.

I started rummaging and found the bundles of photos too. I flicked through some. It always made me happy to see Elvi and Arturo on their journey into the rainforest, and excited too, knowing what they were going to find at the end. I wanted to run through the tangled paths towards them and shout, 'Keep going. Keep going. You're nearly there.'

Then there were the photos Elvi took later, back in her garden. When the seed she'd brought back with her had finally grown into the dragon-fruit tree. Ten years she'd patiently waited. So I could only imagine how excited she must have felt when the tree finally started producing fruit – and dragons! I pored over the pictures of the little dragons perched on her hand or captured flitting among bushes. And then I put them to one side and picked up Elvi's diary.

For a long time there was just the sound of munching and pages being turned as we read.

Then Grandad came in, wondering if he could help. He ended up by helping himself to cake and biscuits!

Ted, licking his lips, suddenly nodded to Kai. 'What have you got there?'

Kai had been riffling through a box and held up a small black canister. 'I don't know.' He prised the lid off and shook out the contents.

'It's a roll of film,' Grandad said. 'From back in the olden days,' he added, with a grin and an eye-roll when we still looked flummoxed. 'Don't suppose you've ever come across one of them. Now you've got cameras in your phones and watches and whatnot. Hold the film up to the light – you'll be able to see better what the photos are of.'

Kai unravelled the roll of film and squinted at the little squares.

'Hey, I think it's Elvi in Mexico. And there's Arturo too.'

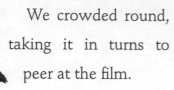

We crowded round, taking it in turns to peer at the film.

'January 1978,' Grandad said, reading a date from the bottom of the canister. He laughed and shook his head. 'And already feels like an antique.'

'Hang on,' I said, quickly flicking back through Elvi's diary to something I had just read. 'What was that date?'

'January 1978,' he replied.

I grabbed the film from a surprised Kai, my eyes darting down the tiny pictures. It was definitely Arturo. Everyone was looking at me now so I must have been jiggling like Lolli when she gets excited.

'This is Elvi and Arturo in Mexico. In 1978. So that photo was taken three months *after* Arturo went missing,' I explained, pointing to the date on the diary entry.

'So you mean he didn't just disappear into the forest, never to be seen again?' Ted said.

'No,' I said with a grin. 'No, he didn't.'

'Elvi went back and found him,' Kat said delightedly.

'But there are no more letters from him,' Kai said, motioning to the piles of papers. 'Surely they'd have kept in touch afterwards, so where is it all?'

'That,' I said, 'is exactly what *I* want to know.'

Elvi had hidden these notebooks under the floorboards in Grandad's shed. But maybe that wasn't the only secret hiding place she had?

We were all jiggling now. Who knew what else we might find?

17

Bang Goes the Superhero Squad

'Let's start looking straight away,' I said excitedly.

Grandad chuckled and got up. 'I think I might leave you lot to it,' he said. 'Just don't go pulling the house to bits while you're hunting.'

I looked around at the others, but everyone had gone a bit quiet.

'Sorry, Tomas,' Liam said. 'I've actually got to get going. Dad's expecting me to help clear the allotment. And Ted said he'd help too,' he added, looking at Ted. 'You know, given that it's for Sunny's benefit.'

Ted gave me an awkward shrug. 'You know what Sunny's like,' he said. 'I want some fruit and veg for him when he visits. Our garden's too small.'

'Oh, right,' I said, wondering when they had been planning to tell me about this.

'So just us then,' I said, turning to Kat and Kai.

Kat gave Kai one of the looks that had been passing between them all week.

'What is up with you two?' I said, letting the disappointment at being left out of Ted and Liam's plan squirm its way out of me. 'Is there something going on we should all know about?'

Kai gave Kat a little nod. 'I think it's time we told them,' he said.

'Told us what?' Liam asked.

'Yeah,' I said. 'Told us what?'

'The thing is . . .' Kat said looking nervous.

'We're moving to China!' Kai blurted excitedly.

He was grinning now, as if relieved that the secret he'd been keeping was finally out in the world.

There was a moment of stunned silence while Kat and Kai looked expectantly at us.

'Mum's been offered this amazing job,' Kat explained quickly. 'In Suzhou, near Shanghai.'

'And Dad can work anywhere,' Kai continued.

'And best of all, we'll get to meet loads of Dad's family – even he hasn't met some of his mum's relatives. Nǎinai left a sister behind when she married Grandpa Jack and moved here.'

'Mum and Dad decided it's too good an opportunity to miss. We're all going to live there, probably for a year or two, maybe more. It's going to be epic!'

'So, what do you think?' Kat asked.

I was too stunned to answer, but Ted and Liam were on board quick as a flash.

'Sounds amazing!' Ted said.

'Awesome!' added Liam.

Kat looked at me. I felt considerably less bouncy. More like a whoopee cushion that's been sat on and deflated.

'Yeah, great,' I said feebly.

I felt as if I'd gone from the top of a roller coaster to the bottom in a split second. And now my stomach was left trying to prise itself off the floor.

'You OK, love?' Mum asked as she kissed me goodnight later on. She felt the back of my neck. 'Not feeling too well?'

I gave a little shrug.

She sat down next to me and stroked a finger down my nose, like it was a tiny ski run. She landed it on the quilt and started doing a two-finger jig of victory.

'Kat and Kai are leaving,' I said quietly.

She gave me a squeeze. 'I know, love. Their mum told me a few days ago. But she said the twins were trying to find the right time to tell you. Not really a right time to hear that though, is there?'

Her fingers skipped up to my chin and tickled it.

'China feels a long way away. It'll be weird not having the twins popping in every five minutes.'

I didn't answer, in case all the mess of feelings inside leaked out.

'That's the great thing about technology though,' she added. 'You can chat to someone on the other side of the world.'

I shook my head, remembering the excited talk that had come after the twins' revelation. The awesome plans they had for once they were living there, showing us pictures of places they would visit and explaining about time differences.

'Not when they're eight hours ahead,' I said sadly. 'When I get back from school, it'll be the middle of the night for them. We'll only be able to talk at the weekend, and that's if they're not off "having adventures". It's the end of the superhero squad.'

Mum bent down and kissed me.

'There's more to the superhero squad than geography, my love.'

I think from my silence she knew I wasn't convinced.

'We'll talk about it some more in the morning. Sweet dreams.'

18
A Flicker of Light

My dreams weren't sweet though. They pinched and poked at me, making me toss and turn. I saw Kat and Kai waving from an aeroplane, Ted and Liam laughing as they ran away together, me standing alone, watching. Let's face it – if my brain had its own weather forecast it would've been 'gloomy with gales and heavy rain'.

I woke up with a shiver and peered into the darkness of my room. The curtains were billowing in the breeze from the window I'd left ajar.

Suddenly there was a flash of light and a huge shadow filled the wall. I scrambled out of bed, threw back the curtains and flung the window wide open, joy bubbling up inside me, like the forecaster had just thrown little suns across the weather map.

'Flicker!'

He pushed his head in through the window and I wrapped my arms around him, his warmth spreading through me.

I climbed out onto Flicker's back, already picturing flying through the star-sparkling night. I knew that the heaviness of my tired arms and the messy tangle of my dreams would quickly fall away and leave me feeling clear-headed and weightless.

Flicker paused and gazed back into my room, I turned to look. Zing. I'd completely forgotten. He'd rocketed back in through the window just before I'd fallen asleep. I'd been too weary to even get up and deal with the mug of water he'd sent flying. I'd just watched him disappear into his nest under my bed, but now he'd woken up and was spinning in circles round the room. Flicker blew a smoky breath that

spread like a guiding path and the little dragon flew out of the dizzy loop he was spiralling in and followed the smoke trail towards us.

It was a cloudy night, and as we flew higher I scanned the sky for the other dragons. But there was no sign of them. As we left the village it was soon clear that for once Flicker was on his own. He soared higher and we burst out into the star-pricked midnight-blue night. For a while we just flew. Flicker's wings beating slow and steady, his scales settling into a turquoise gleam. I breathed deep and reached out my arms as if I could touch the stars.

Zing darted over Flicker's head and then started flying in a corkscrew loop down the big dragon's body, getting faster and faster as he approached the end of his tail. He definitely seemed excited to see Flicker. When he did finally settle on the very tip of his tail, Flicker flicked the little dragon into the air, only to swish his tail and catch him again. Zing seemed to love this, letting out crackles and sparks as he spun through the air. I guess it was like us bouncing on a trampoline.

Flicker dipped his head and roared, unleashing a mighty blue flame. And I smiled and clung on as we sped through the night.

However magical it was flying with Flicker though, somehow it just wasn't the same without all of us there. And by the time we finally flew home and I climbed back in through the window, I felt chilled despite Flicker's warm scales.

As Zing darted in and disappeared under my bed, I turned and stared into Flicker's diamond eyes. Colours danced and fragmented as I felt his gaze reaching into the heart of me.

'Kat and Kai are leaving,' I blurted. And then, in more sob than words, I added, 'There'll be no more superhero squad without them.'

And the whole sorry story tumbled out. When I eventually ran out of words and all that was left was hiccupy sobs, Flicker let out a deep low rumble that went on for the longest time. It shook the tears right out of me, until I finally felt my body relax.

Flicker blew a puff of smoke that crackled with blue sparks, lighting up my room. Then he leaned his head against me and nudged me towards my bed. I crawled under the covers and lay there watching the sparks dancing and twinkling above me. He let out another puff, his gaze fixed on me, warming me.

Puff. Spark. Twinkle. Puff. Spark. Twinkle. Repeat. Until my eyelids began to droop.

And this time my dreams were sweet. I was with Zing, being carried on Flicker's tail, laughing as he sent us rocketing into the air, spiralling upwards and diving down, only to catch us up again. We crossed paths mid-air like juggling balls. And then finally he brought us back to Grandad's garden. And with one last gentle tilt of his tail he sent the pair of us rolling into deep soft grass, Zing tumbling into my lap.

When I woke up I felt warm. I pulled back the covers and stared down at the source of this toastiness. There curled up next to me was Zing, fast asleep. For the first time he had wriggled his way in and tucked himself beside me. His huge wings lay across me, the silver threads only faintly visible now as they rose and fell with my tummy.

19
Zapow!

Not wanting to disturb the sleeping dragon, I inched my way out of bed. It was early but I could hear Lolli singing away in her room. As well as the mug Zing had sent flying, I saw that he'd also made a complete mess of the bundle of photos I'd brought back from Grandad's. They'd been scattered across the floor. I started gathering them up, relieved that at least he hadn't shredded them for his nest. Most of them were photos of Elvi's garden, when the dragons were finally growing. But one caught my eye. It was a photo of Elvi herself, standing by the dragon-fruit tree. She was cradling something in her arms. And it wasn't a dragon. It was a baby.

I turned the photo over and saw her scribbly writing: 'Sweet Rosa, 1979'.

I stared at the little baby, and then at Elvi. We'd always thought Elvi had been on her own growing dragons. But looking at this photo, it was clear we hadn't known the whole story. I tucked the photo into my pocket. I couldn't wait to show the others.

I scooped up Zing and crept along the corridor to Lolli's room.

'Don't get him excited,' I warned. 'I'm just clearing up the last mess he made.'

She nodded dutifully.

Back in my room I dashed around putting things to rights and checking for any hidden poos. There were none, thank goodness. Zing still hadn't eaten anything

I'd offered him, but I assumed he must be finding food of some sort. Then I spent a fiddly half-hour reattaching scales to my dragon costume and adding some last-minute cardboard-cone spines to the body.

When I headed back to Lolli's room, I found her bouncing round the bathroom, her hair sticking up and out at all angles. She giggled when she saw me, and then she flung out her arm and cried out: 'Powee!'

'You OK, Lollibob?' I grinned, my eyes darting about to check Zing was still in her room and not on the loose.

'Lolli got superpower!' she cried. 'Lolli zappy powee power.'

And she pointed her finger at the lampshade, as if something might blast from the end of it.

I joined in and zapped the light too.

'Zapow!' I cried.

She stopped and looked a bit cross. 'There's not nuffink in your finger,' she said. 'Only Lolli finger got the zap.'

She looked at me again and added, 'But you can pretend if you like.'

I was about to say that I needed to go and check on Zing, when I saw it wasn't a doll or a teddy in the baby carrier she had strapped to her. Along with Stefan, the still-bandaged wooden spoon, I could see the silver tip of Zing's tail peeking out.

'Has he been OK?' I asked, pointing to the little dragon.

'Zing got a bit over-'cited,' she said quietly. She rested a hand protectively on him and then bit her lip. 'He's probably sorry.'

I quickly headed for her room. There was paint all over her carpet. Lolli had obviously done her best to clear it up, but having failed to make it disappear she'd opted to spread it vaguely into the shape of a dragon instead.

Luckily Mum and Dad didn't seem to notice the mess Zing was making around the house. They'd been far too busy planning their next video, lining up which animals Dad could safely record, and dealing with the family of terrapins, the tarantula and the bearded lizard Mum had volunteered to look after for one of our neighbours. They were so busy, in fact, that they'd actually forgotten to cook the bolognaise part of our spaghetti bolognaise tea the previous evening. So it was just spaghetti. Ketchup spaghetti in mine and Lolli's case.

I opened Lolli's window, and as we headed downstairs for breakfast, Zing darted out. Later, on the way to school, I spotted him zipping from treetop to treetop, keeping his sapphire eye on me.

After all the extra work I'd put in on my dragon costume, I was pretty pleased with the overall effect. And I was looking forward to roaring my way through the school gates. Sadly, by the time I got to school, I'd lost most of the spines and quite a few of the scales.

I looked around the playground and saw that Aura was already there in her costume. A crowd of excited children had gathered around her, the superhero squad among them. My shoulders sagged as I noticed she'd added more colour to it by fashioning an even longer tail, that she'd attached to her hand with string so she could swish it back and forth. I wished I'd thought of that. My own tail trailing behind me had already been stepped on about three times and was looking limp and flattened.

I ground to a halt. A small Year One boy squinted up at me, looking puzzled.

'Are you a robot?' he asked.

'I'm a dragon,' I said flatly.

He shook his head. 'I don't think so,' he said. 'That's a dragon.' And he pointed at Aura. 'I think you're a robot.'

'Well, I'm not,' I said.

He shrugged. 'Bye-bye, robot.'

20
Queen of the Dragons

I shuffled into class past the rest of my classmates, who'd mostly decided to come as unicorns and had stuck a range of pointy things to their heads, with varying success. The only non-unicorns were Ted who'd come as a Cyclops, Kat and Kai as Medusa and a merman and Liam as a pretty impressive-looking Poseidon. Oh and the Minotaur in the corner, who I think was Mahid, though it was hard to tell under the papier mâché head.

Miss Jelinski gave a round of applause as we settled into our seats.

'Well done on your costumes, everyone,' she said. 'I can see that you have all made tremendous efforts. Right, before we carry on writing our own legends, since I wasn't here earlier in the week to greet her properly I thought we'd spend a little time getting to know our newest member of the class. Aura, would you like to come and tell us a little bit about yourself? And indeed your costume. It really is wonderful and we'd love to hear all about it – and you.'

Aura bounded out to the front of the class, grinning. She reminded me of Tigger out of *Winnie-the-Pooh*. And maybe a bit of Zing too, especially when her bounding nearly sent Miss Jelinski's mug of water flying. You could almost feel the buzz coming off her as she stood there.

'I'm Aura,' she said. Then she added, with an elaborate wave of her hand, 'But you can call me Queen of the Dragons.'

I think Miss Jelinski might have underestimated how much Aura had to tell us about herself – and about dragons. She certainly liked to show off what she knew. So it was almost morning break by the time we were ready to get on with our writing.

When the bell went and the rest of the class bundled outside, I managed to signal to the superhero squad to wait. I was eager to seize my chance and show them the photo of Elvi I'd found, but then Aura came running back into class, clutching a bag.

'Hey,' she said, 'I've got this awesome dragon ring. Do you want to see it?'

She stretched out her hand and showed us the silver ring, a dragon coiling round her index finger.

'That really is awesome,' said Liam.

'And that's not all,' she said excitedly. 'I've brought loads of dragon stuff to show you.'

We crowded round as she started rummaging in her rucksack, pulling things out and handing them to us. There was a pen with a dragon wrapped around the end, a pencil case covered in dragon scales, a really cool dragon pendant necklace and a leather-style notebook which had a little dragon as the clasp, its claw sealing any secrets written inside.

'These things are so cool,' Kai said.

And he was right, they really were.

'I know all there is to know about dragons,' Aura said proudly. 'I have the best dragon book at home; it tells you *everything* about them. Go on, ask me anything.'

We all looked at each other, not quite knowing what to say.

'Try me, go on.'

But before any of us could reply, Mrs Muddleton, our head teacher, appeared in the doorway and started shepherding us out to the playground.

'If only she knew, hey?' Kai whispered to me, as Kat linked arms with Aura and hurried her along.

'Aura's certainly read a lot of books about dragons,' Ted said at home time.

'Yeah,' agreed Kai. 'She even out-facted you there, Ted. Who knew that when people first discovered dinosaur bones they thought they belonged to dragons!'

'I don't know *all* the facts,' Ted said a bit sulkily.

'Neither does Aura,' I pointed out, aware that Ted was looking a bit like a deflated balloon. 'I mean, however much you read about them in books, she doesn't *really* know about dragons, does she?'

'Maybe we should fill her in then,' said Liam. 'We could show her *exactly* what dragons are like.'

Kat smiled and looked as if she might be about to agree with him.

'No way,' I said quickly. 'It's meant to be a secret. *Our* secret. We can't be blurting it out.'

You know how, looking back, sometimes you say things that later on you wish you could forget you'd said? That was one I'd want to forget I said pretty soon.

21
Jam Tarts and Warrior Spiders

On the way home from school we promised each other that first thing on Saturday we'd start the search for Arturo's missing letters. Once I'd shown them the photograph of Elvi with her baby, I think everyone realised there was a lot we still didn't know.

I'd been full of hope for the seedlings after meeting Chouko. But her advice about putting holes in the pots and sprinkling them with worm poo wasn't working. Two more of the seedlings had died and a couple of others were looking floppy, their leaves shrivelled and brown. It felt more important than ever to find out if Arturo had anything else to tell us.

On Saturday morning, while I waited for the superhero squad to arrive, Lolli jumped at the chance to use my arms and legs for bandage practice – until Mum came in and saw quite how much toilet roll we'd used.

As she bundled Lolli off to her swimming lesson, I once again tried to perk up the seedlings.

I remembered how Grandad's neighbour, Jim, had played music to his plants, encouraging them to grow. I had no idea if it would actually work, but I figured I had to try everything.

'I reckon you might be doing more harm than good there,' Ted said as he came into my room. I quickly stopped my pitiful strumming of 'Three Blind Mice' on my ukulele.

He smiled and added, 'Still no luck with the seedlings then?'

I shook my head. 'We lost two more,' I said sadly.

'Well, let's hope we're right about there being more to find out from Arturo,' he said.

'Where are the others?' I asked, looking past him.

'Liam had to help in the allotment and Kat and Kai sent an SOS saying they've been ordered to clear out their bedrooms for the big move. So it's just us.'

'Right,' I said, trying not to feel disappointed. 'We'd better go then.'

By the time we got to Nana and Grandad's I'd convinced myself we were moments away from another great discovery. I couldn't wait to get into the shed and start looking. But thanks to Ted's stomach, not before we'd eaten some much-needed provisions.

'Your nana really does make the best jam tarts,' Ted said, one hand reaching into Grandad's goodies tin as the other stuffed a third tart into his mouth.

I nodded and licked the last of the gooseberry jam off my fingers.

I'd given up offering titbits to Zing – whatever he was finding to eat, it wasn't anything I'd offered him. He had perched on Grandad's radio and I was glad that for once he wasn't crashing into or breaking anything.

'Shall we have a look then?' I said. 'I've got a good feeling about this. Just keep an eye out for warrior spiders,' I shuddered, as I remembered the beast I'd found guarding the hiding place the first time.

Ted, who was even less happy about coming face to face with creepy-crawlies, leaped up onto Grandad's stool.

'The view's better from up here,' he said sheepishly.

I moved aside the boxes covering the floorboard with the metal ring and then ducked back down. The space where the tin with the notebooks had been hidden wasn't huge, but this time I was determined to check thoroughly that I hadn't missed something.

I lifted the board and reached my hand in, groping around, my fingernails scratching at the soil.

Zing flew down and joined me, whacking me in the face with one of his wings as he did.

'Any luck?' Ted said, peering down.

'No, nothing,' I said.

I began to clear more space under the counter, keen to see if there could be another secret hidey-hole. I thought we'd found something when Ted jumped off the stool shrieking, but it turned out a butterfly had just fluttered past his hair.

'This shed makes me jumpy,' he said.

'You're not the only one,' I replied, watching Zing fly frantically along the wall.

'I don't think there's anything else in here,' I said at last with a sigh. I sat back on my heels, brushing the cobwebs off my arms. 'And I think we should probably get out before Zing starts bashing into stuff.'

Ted didn't need persuading. He was out the door in a flash, as was Zing, who immediately began dive-bombing a heap of compost piled up next to the side of the shed, burrowing into it and flinging clods everywhere.

'Maybe Elvi had other hiding places,' Ted suggested, still looking himself over for any creepy-crawlies who might have hitched a ride.

'Up to the house then, I guess,' I replied.

'Actually, Tomas, I did say I'd go and help Liam,' Ted said, looking at his watch.

I felt my body do the sag and slump, like a ball that's had all the air kicked out of it.

'You should come too,' he added. 'In between the digging, we usually have a laugh. The snacks aren't up to your nana's standards, but I've still got a stash of sherbet and Liam's mum always gives us a massive bag of crisps to share.'

'I can't,' I said. 'I promised I'd stay and help out here once I was done hunting.'

I watched Ted as he headed up the garden path. He turned when he reached the house and gave me a final wave before disappearing.

'Looks like it's just you and me then,' I said, glancing over at Zing. But with his head half buried in the compost heap he couldn't even hear me.

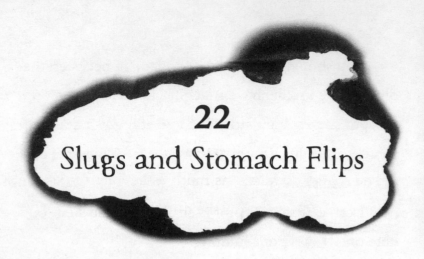

22
Slugs and Stomach Flips

On Monday we went into school, only to discover Miss Jelinski was off sick. A long week with Mr Firth loomed like a thunderous black cloud over our heads. On top of that, another three seedlings had died. But I couldn't share my worries with the superhero squad because Ted kept going off with Liam on special missions to grow food for their dragons, and the twins were busy getting ready for their move. And then there was Aura, popping up all the time, so even when I did have the superhero squad all together, we were never on our own.

For someone small, she took up quite a lot of space. Apart from flinging her arms about whenever she spoke, her voice always ended up being the loudest in our little group. None of the others seemed to mind. Kat had taken charge of Aura – as much as anyone could take charge of her – as soon as she'd arrived. They'd hit it off immediately and now always sat together.

I still couldn't believe that the superhero squad hadn't met Zing! But I could never predict when he would be around. He was always disappearing and then reappearing somewhere else. And with Aura tagging along with us after school, it was too risky anyway.

On Friday morning I woke up feeling as if a monstrous slug had slept on me, squishing me flat. Not even the fact that it was the last day before half-term could unsquish me. I peeled myself off the bed and dragged myself into school.

At first my spirits rose as I saw the superhero squad huddled in the corner of the playground, for once minus Aura. But then I heard what they were saying.

'You tell him,' said Liam.

'No, you tell him,' Ted hissed.

'It'll be better coming from you.'

'It was Kat who did it – she should tell him,' Kai said.

They all turned to look at Kat, and then noticed that she was no longer looking at them. She was looking at me.

'Tell me what?' I asked, eyes darting between the four of them.

For a moment everyone looked at everyone else and no one said anything.

Then Kat elbowed Kai and said, 'I wouldn't have had to do anything if you and Liam hadn't been too busy trying to beat each other in that race to notice what was going on.'

'What was going on?' I hissed. 'And what race?'

This last question made the whole superhero squad shuffle uncomfortably.

Eventually Ted filled me in.

'Our dragons came back last night.'

'Hang on. What? They came back?' I said. My stomach did an Olympics-worthy backflip as the inevitable question popped into my head. Then why hadn't Flicker come?

'Er . . . yeah.' Ted looked awkward as he watched my stricken face. 'We thought perhaps you and Flicker were off somewhere. You know, on your own.'

I shook my head and Ted went quiet. I immediately thought of Zing, curled up next to me in my bed. And my heart suddenly felt like it was being squeezed. What if Flicker had turned up and seen the little dragon with me and felt left out? Maybe he thought I didn't need him any more. So he'd flown away.

'Maxi and Dodger started racing,' Kat said. 'And Dodger took this shortcut and it took him close to the village hall. Only there was someone outside. We don't know if they actually spotted him. But even if they didn't, it was too close.'

'Which is why Kat ordered the dragons to stay away,' Kai explained.

'I didn't have a choice,' Kat said desperately. 'I told Crystal they all need to keep a low profile, just for a bit, in case anyone did see something and starts looking more closely.'

'You told Crystal that?' I asked.

She nodded sadly. 'It won't have to be forever, Tomas. Just until it's safe for them.'

'That's all well and good,' said Liam, breaking the silence that followed, 'but how do we let them know it's safe? They might never come back.'

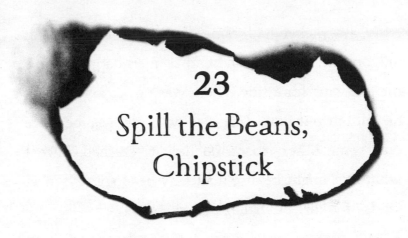

23
Spill the Beans, Chipstick

You know when you wake up and think it's the weekend and then you get that blast of disappointment when you realise it's actually a Tuesday. Well, for once I had that feeling when I woke up on an actual Saturday. And what's more, a Saturday at the start of a school holiday. Not because I suddenly had extra holiday lessons of grammar with Mr Firth (although how nightmarish would that be?) but because my head was full of worries about Flicker. My dragon hadn't come to me in the night. Not even in my dreams.

I kept telling myself that I was wrong to worry.

After all, Flicker had come back without the other dragons once himself and had seemed happy to take me and Zing for a ride. There was no reason to think he felt left out now Zing was with me. Maybe there was some other reason he hadn't returned. Except what that might be also made my head spin off in all kinds of wildly unsettling directions.

Of course now Kat had told the dragons to keep away, I had no way of finding out the truth. And the trouble was, I couldn't get rid of the little worm in my ear. The one muttering, 'What if Liam is right? What if they never come back?'

When I got to Nana and Grandad's I found Grandad happily pruning some roses and whistling away.

'You OK, Chipstick?' he said, seeing me. 'Ready to do battle with the wreckage? You're right about dragons being a lot more trouble than cucumbers! One of them keeps making a right old mess of my raspberry nets.'

He looked around for the others.

'Hang on, where's the rest of the bunch?'

'Busy,' I said flatly.

'What are they so busy with?'

'Stuff.'

Grandad nodded. 'Bloomin' stuff. It don't half get in the way sometimes.'

He wasn't wrong there. My grand plans for half-term had been well and truly flattened thanks to Kat and Kai being whisked away to visit relatives all week, Liam staying in Scotland with his granny and Ted on a week's barge holiday in France.

'Give us a sec and I'll give you a hand,' Grandad said.

'It's fine,' I replied. 'I'll manage.'

I started picking up beanpoles and flowerpots that had been knocked flying, muttering to myself.

Grandad said sometimes the best way to get rid of a grump is with a bit of elbow grease. Meaning get busy with a job and you'd soon forget to be cross.

But I wasn't convinced elbow grease would work this time.

After half an hour of tidying and grumbling away to myself, this grump was bigger and badder than ever. A great big smelly toad of a grump that squatted on the ground, girruping grump slime over everything I touched.

'Right, Chipstick,' Grandad said. 'Enough's enough. Spill those beans.'

'What beans?' I said, looking around the garden.

'The ones you're carrying around, that are weighing you down. Come on – time for a biscuit and a natter. You can tell me what's got you looking like a wet weekend.'

So as Grandad headed into the shed to fetch the tin and a flask of sweet milky tea, I put down my spade and perched on the old bench.

When he came back he held out the tin, crammed with home-made ginger biscuits and squares of flapjack. I took one of each, resting them on my knees as I warmed my hands around the mug of tea he'd poured for me. For a minute or two he just left me alone to drink my tea and nibble on my biscuit. There was never any rush with Grandad. And maybe that's why I always ended up telling him in the end.

'Why do things have to change?' I said quietly.

Grandad gave a chuckle. 'Well, that's a pretty big question for elevenses.' He handed me another biscuit.

'Things were great,' I said. 'I've got four best friends. We grow dragons. We even ride dragons. We do everything together and we always have. Why does it have to go and change?'

'I'm guessing you're not too happy about Kat and Kai upping sticks and moving away?'

'It's bad enough having a week without them all here. What am I going to do when they leave for good?'

'Your little band of buddies has been through a lot together. They're a good bunch.'

'The best,' I said. 'Or we were.'

'And you still are – and will be,' Grandad said. 'No question about that. You don't need to be in each other's pockets for that to be true. Good friends stick.'

'I know, I know – like jam tarts,' I said.

'Absolutely. But you're right, things do change. Nothing stays the same forever.'

'But why can't it?' I said. 'I want it to.'

Grandad scooched closer and put his arm round my shoulder, giving me a squeeze.

'Look at this garden,' he said. 'What have we grown? Radishes, beans, strawberries, onions, raspberries, leeks, lettuces . . . oh, and a few dragons. And what have they all got in common?'

I dug my foot down into a clod of mud and shrugged.

'They all grew,' he said. 'If nothing changed, nothing would grow. And things need to grow. Even us.'

24
The Big Red Button

By the end of the afternoon, thanks to a combination of biscuits, digging and Grandad's twinkliness shining on me, I felt a good deal better. But sadly it didn't last.

I was just passing the little playground by the village hall when Aura ran up and roared at me. I was concentrating so hard on how to keep the superhero squad together long distance that I pretty much jumped into the hedge.

'Sorry about that,' she said, pulling a twig out of my hair. 'You're ever so jumpy.'

'Yeah, well, you did just leap out at me,' I said a bit

crossly. 'I was thinking, that's all.'

'Oh, I've been thinking too,' she said. 'I've been thinking that Miss Jelinski is totally wrong.'

I sighed. We'd had days of Aura trying to convince Miss Jelinski and Mr Firth that in the school play of Little Red Riding Hood we should update it and have a dragon rather than a wolf. The dragon to be played by Aura, of course.

'It's all that Mr Firth's fault. Miss Jelinski loves dragons almost as much as I do. I bet she'd let me if she could. If we all asked they'd have to say yes. What do you think? Do you reckon we can start a class petition?'

'I doubt Mr Firth would listen even if the Queen asked him,' I said, really hoping she'd stop going on about it.

'Well, I'm the Queen of Dragons, so maybe he'll listen to me. And I'd do a brilliant job. Miss Jelinski already told me I know more about dragons than anyone she's ever met.'

I know I shouldn't have cared, but this really bugged me. I carried on walking though.

'I mean, apart from already having the costume,' Aura went on proudly, spreading her imaginary wings. 'Dragons are way more fierce and scary than a silly old wolf – anyone knows that.'

I stopped and turned to face her.

'Actually that's not true.'

'Course it is. I've read all the books. Dragons are fierce.'

'No, they're not.'

'Are too.'

'Are not.'

I suddenly felt as if I was channelling my inner Lolli, all set to stamp my feet at her. Honestly, she had been doing this ever since she'd arrived, acting like a complete know-it-all.

'You don't know everything about dragons, you know,' I said.

'Course I do. I've always loved dragons. I've got

more books and toys and dragon stuff than anyone.'

'That doesn't mean you know everything. I know stuff too. And I *know* that not all dragons are fierce.'

She frowned and took a deep breath as if she was going to have to be really patient with a very small and annoying person.

'You're just jealous,' she said simply. She turned to walk away, nose in the air, then looked back over her shoulder and added, 'And wrong.'

You know when someone just presses that button on your head – the big red button that sets off all the alarms and stuff? And you feel as if your whole body

has been blasted with fiery heat and it wants to shoot out of you, and if it doesn't you are going to explode.

Well, Aura had just pressed That Button.

Instead of actually exploding though, I said the one thing I really, *really* shouldn't have.

'You know what?' I spluttered. '*You're* wrong. And what's more, I can prove it.'

25
King of the Dragons

Now what I should have done was rush after those words that had barged their way out, scoop them up and jam them back in my mouth. And then I should have kept it well and truly shut.

But I didn't. At that moment all I wanted to do was prove to Aura how wrong she was. I was going to show her exactly who was Grand High DragonMaster round here. I stomped my way home, Aura hurrying along behind, asking over and over again what I meant by that.

'You'll see,' is all I said.

She followed me into the house, not even blinking when we passed Mum, Dad and Lolli in the hall, their hair sticking up like they'd all been wrestling their way out of a hedge, which given that Mum was cradling an angry-looking Tomtom, maybe they had.

Upstairs, I flung my bedroom door open, marched over to my bed and crouched down. Spotting Zing curled up and sleeping, I pointed in triumph at the little dragon.

Aura, too far away to see him, looked at me like I was completely barmy. I pointed again, knowing that any second she was going to be eating her words with a big slice of toasted humble pie and sprinklings of sorry.

She took a step towards me, dodging the scattered piles of Lego, the shredded wreckage of six of my comics and what I suddenly realised was a pair of my scorched pants. I darted forward and kicked them behind my beanbag, hoping she hadn't seen.

When I turned back, she was leaning down, peering under the bed, her mouth hanging open.

'It's . . . it's . . . it's
. . . a dragon,' she finally
stammered.

'Yup,' I said, satisfied.
'He totally is.'

Before I could stop her,
Aura had leaned in further,
her hand reaching out to
touch the little sleeping
dragon. Zing's sapphire
eye snapped open and,
seeing the outstretched
fingers and Aura's
face peering at
him, he practically
exploded out from
under the bed. Like he
was turbo-charged. He rocketed up to the ceiling
and began flapping round in frantic loops, wings
crashing into things and sending out crackling sparks.

'This is unreal,' she said as she watched him. 'Like totally, pinch me, whack me round the face with a wet fish, tell me I'm dreaming, unreal.'

I couldn't help but give a snort of laughter at that.

'And totally, utterly, mind-bendingly awesome,' she added, grinning. And she ducked as Zing batted a Lego model off my shelf and sent it flying and crashing into the wall.

'How?' she said. 'How is this possible?'

'Dragons aren't just in stories, you know,' I said.

She paused for a second and then, looking serious, mimed taking something off her head. She handed the something to me, reverently. And when I looked bemused, she motioned for me to take it.

'My crown,' she said. 'I think we have a new *King* of the Dragons.'

Strangely, hearing her say that didn't feel quite as good as I'd hoped.

The trouble was, I hadn't planned to reveal the secret that I had a dragon. It was a blurt. An uncontrolled blurt. And that lump of blurt was now lying leaden in my stomach, heavier than Mum's jam roly-poly pudding. I knew the superhero squad would be furious with me for telling Aura. Especially after I'd made such a big deal out of saying that we shouldn't. If there was still a superhero squad, then had I just risked being booted out of it?

'So, tell me,' she said, flopping onto my bed, her eyes not leaving Zing for a second. 'I want to know *everything.*'

The thing I was discovering about Aura was that she was persistent. Actually scrap that. *Very* persistent. *And* good at getting her way. She also made me feel like I actually was King of the Dragons and should have a crown.

So without meaning to, I may have told her a few things – about the dragon-fruit tree, and how I found it in Grandad's garden, and about Flicker.

Big flappy mouth that I have. At least I stopped myself before I got to the bit about Elvi and how we all started growing dragons, and about Liam's super-sizing adventures, and Lolli growing Tinkle. But if I thought not mentioning the others having dragons would help, I was wrong.

Because a second later, she said exactly what Ted had said the first day he'd met Flicker. And just like that, my stomach did a lolloping lurch. And if you don't remember what that was, just imagine what you would say if you were shown a dragon and told they grow on trees. Yup, you got it.

'Hey, can I grow one too then?'

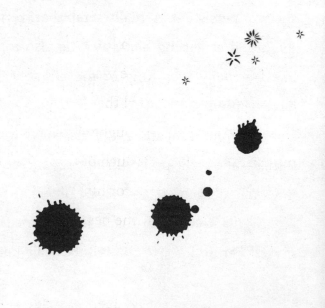

26
That's Magic!

Aura sat watching me as I wrestled with the thoughts that were whirling around inside my head. She positively zinged with excitement, just like Zing in fact.

'Well?' she said. 'Can I? Can I?'

The answer of course was no – we'd been through all that and we'd learned that keeping dragons wasn't good for them or us. Though with Zing flapping round my room I didn't have much of a leg to stand on. But it wasn't like I'd intended for him to stay.

'Pleeeeeeeeaaase,' she begged again.

I could tell she wouldn't stop asking. I thought

about the last crop of dragons hatching and how there wouldn't be any ripe fruit now, not for a little while.

'I'll show you the tree tomorrow,' I said finally.

Aura gave a whoop of delight and started dancing round the room, sending Zing off on another frenzied bout of somersaults.

She obviously had the same turbo-boost setting as Zing. And I knew that in the long run I'd need the superhero squad to back me up. Of course, for that to happen, I'd have to admit that I'd blurted out the truth about the dragons. My stomach did a little undulation, like a blubbery seal flolloping over the ice. And as Aura skipped off home – and that's not a joke; she actually skipped with joy like Lolli does – the seal slid miserably into the frozen depths, taking my stomach with it.

'Hello,' said Nana as I brought Aura into their kitchen the next day. 'There's a face I haven't seen before.'

'I'm Aura.' She smiled. 'That smells delicious.' She leaned over the pan Nana was stirring.

'Well, now, the amount Tomas's grandad grows, I needed a plan. And that plan,' she chortled, 'is jam. There's only so much crumble this lot can eat. Me and Lolli are going to sell it at the school fête this year – I'm sure we'll raise lots of money for charity. Everyone loves jam.'

'Sounds like a great plan to me,' Aura said.

'Where's Grandad?' I asked.

'He's off on a mission to find some more worms. I'd have thought there'd be enough in that there garden. But he had his own plan.'

Leaving Nana to her jammy exploits, I led Aura out the back door and down the path towards the crooked apple trees.

'That jam smells amazing,' she said dreamily. 'I love your nana's kitchen. It's really . . .' she paused, searching for the word, 'friendly.'

I smiled, remembering all the family meals we'd had round the table, Nana heaping our plates with

Sunday roasts, stew and dumplings and sweet sticky puddings. The amount of custard we'd consumed in that room would probably fill a lake. I wandered into my own dream of creamy yellow waterfalls flowing over plains of crumble and boulders of chocolate sponge.

'I see what your nana means about all the fruit,' Aura said pointing at the trees. 'And look – a blackthorn tree. You should pick the sloes – blackberry and sloe jam is delicious.'

'Grandad would be impressed – I didn't know what a sloe was until I started working in his garden.'

Aura suddenly looked puzzled.

'Do you know,' she said, 'I impress myself sometimes. I didn't even know I knew what a sloe was. It's funny – this garden reminds me of somewhere. All the fruit trees and beehives.' She gazed around her, suddenly lost in thought.

'Come on,' I said. 'The tree's over here.'

She grinned and skipped over to join me, leaving the fruit trees waving behind us.

Standing in front of the dragon-fruit tree, Aura's face lit up. She stared at the draping cactus leaves and peered in at the hairy trunk. And she grinned madly when I pointed out one of the spiky fruits. Thankfully I'd been right and all the fruits we could see were green, which meant there wouldn't be any dragons hatching for a while yet. I felt myself relax a bit.

'This is the coolest-looking tree *ever*,' she said. 'It looks like you made it up in your head, Tomas.'

I laughed. 'I know. It even has these yellow and orange tendrils that shoot out like a burst of flames. And ginormous moon-white flowers that only bloom for one night.'

'See?' She laughed. 'It's like a fairy-tale tree.'

She leaned in closer and touched one of the fruits gently.

'Except it's real, isn't it? And the dragons are real too.'

I nodded.

'Magic,' she whispered.

And it was exactly at that moment that the fruit she was touching began to glow.

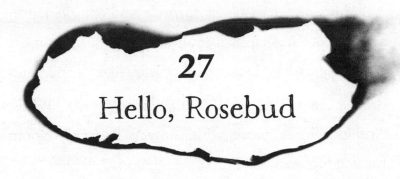

27
Hello, Rosebud

Aura giggled delightedly, while I just gawped at the green fruit. What was going on? Normally the fruits only glowed when they turned red.

The next second the fruit began to bulge and then it dropped from the branch. Aura's hands shot out and caught it. The glow lit up her fingers as she held it out towards me.

'What do I do?' she asked, looking alarmed.

But before I could reply, the fruit burst open and she was splattered with seeds and pulp as a tiny dragon shot out.

She jumped back in surprise and knocked into me just as Zing zipped down from a branch, almost crashing into my head as he flew over us. I tried and failed to keep my balance and ended up on my bottom in the mud.

Meanwhile, the newly hatched dragon landed on the ground in front of us and staggered a bit under the weight of a piece of dragon-fruit skin still stuck to its back. Aura reached down to peel the sticky fruit away, so the little creature could lift its head properly and stretch its wings. For once Aura had gone very quiet – she was just staring at the dragon and its bright little eyes were staring right back.

Aura had got her wish. She had grown a dragon.

Its body was the bright green of new spring grass and its wings a darker peacock green. They weren't the usual bat-wing shape either, they were oval. And they had ridges through them like the veins on a leaf. Its tail was covered in tiny sharp spines like thorns. The dragon raised its head and we watched as two

quite long horns started to glow. Then it saw me and, like an alarmed hedgehog curling into a ball, pulled its wings around itself. But left its spiky tail held out as if it was battle ready.

'That's amazing,' Aura said, finally finding her voice. 'She looks just like a bud. A rosebud. And her tail is the thorny branch.'

She was right. The oval wings enclosed the dragon like the petals on a flower. Aura carefully picked the dragon up and held it close to her face. Ever so gently, she blew over the little creature.

'What are you doing?' I asked.

'My mum used to do it to me when I was little. She always said it calmed me down. I think she got a bit of a shock seeing us there.'

The dragon's wings parted, like a flower opening to the sun, and a little head peeked out.

And Aura gave the biggest grin.

'Hello, Rosebud,' she whispered.

It was soon clear that this little dragon, like Zing, had no intention of just flying off. Despite dragging a protesting Aura away to hide in the shed in the hopes that the dragon might leave, when we re-emerged Rosebud was there waiting on a branch, looking quizzically at us.

It took Rosebud and Zing a little while to get used to each other. At first Rosebud curled up behind her wings every time Zing flapped towards her. Not that I could blame her really – Zing still flew like he was about to crash into you. Eventually though he landed on Grandad's spade. Just as he settled, Rosebud launched up into the air, zipped through the low hanging trees and came up behind him, flicking him with her tail and startling him so much he toppled off. After that they seemed to get on much better.

Sitting in the shed with our dragons perched on the shelf above us, I told Aura about Flicker. How his scales flickered through every colour, shining so brightly, how he shone with bright ideas too, and how it had felt like a fizzling firework was going off inside me when he settled on my shoulder and wrapped his tail around my neck.

Rosebud flew down and landed on Aura's arm, her claws latching on to her jumper. She tucked in her head and tail and pulled her wings around herself. It was as if the dragon was a bud and Aura's arm was the branch.

My eyes flicked towards Zing. Somehow I didn't fancy him curling that silver spiked tail around my

neck, and he was likely to whack me round the ear with his oversized wings anyway.

'Flicker still comes back,' I said, willing myself to believe that this was still the case even after Kat's orders. 'Just wait till you meet him.'

Aura's eyes flicked to Zing and she smiled at him.

'Dragons are the best. You're so lucky to have the dragon-fruit tree in your grandparents' garden.'

I smiled and nodded. Aura hatching a dragon wasn't meant to happen. And when the superhero squad got back from their holidays I was going to have to own up to what I'd done. But even so, it felt good to share the tree with her. To watch someone else seeing the magic happen for the first time.

28
Poo Patrol

'It'll be fine,' Aura said. 'Honestly, after everything you've just told me, I reckon I'm prepared for anything.'

I snorted. 'You can never fully prepare for life with a dragon,' I replied. 'Seriously, you have to keep your eyes wide open. And whatever you do, don't let anyone else see her.'

I wondered for the gazillionth time whether letting Aura go home with Rosebud had been a good idea. It was true I'd explained about using ash, along with clicks and whistles, to teach Rosebud a few basic commands. But given that Zing hadn't shown any interest in it, I couldn't guarantee it would be much help.

At least I could tell her my top tips on the best ways to hide any incriminating evidence – burnt socks, singed homework, shredded newspapers, that sort of thing. And of course I'd described the intricacies of poo patrol, letting her know just how nasty an explosion of the stuff could be.

But could I really trust her?

'We've got this,' Aura said, cradling Rosebud in her hand. 'I promise.'

I really hoped she was right. I watched her head off, my oven glove and water pistol stuffed into her back pockets. Then I looked over at Zing. I still hadn't worked out what he liked to eat and, as far as I could tell, he hadn't yet done a poo. I was beginning to wonder if that was OK.

'Just so you know,' I said warily, 'until Aura gets her own poo-patrol equipment sorted tomorrow, I'm without oven gloves and a water pistol.'

Over tea I tried quizzing Mum about the pooing habits of various animals. But it didn't go down too well.

'Time and a place, Tomas,' Mum said, a forkful of food wavering in front of her face. I guess she had a point.

By the time I'd helped her wash up, I had quite an extensive knowledge. Ted would have been proud. Here are some things I learned. (Note that if you ask a vet, be prepared – you get all the information you wanted and quite a lot more gross stuff too.)

1. Cows can poo sixteen times a day.

A sloth may only poo once a week.

2. Everyone poos, except for the Demodex mite that lives on your face – 'Ew' to a mite living on your face, 'Hurray' that at least it doesn't poo on it.

3. Vultures poo on their feet. Because after standing in rotten stuff all day eating, their feet are covered in germs, and the poo contains bacteria that kill the germs. Personally I don't care how grubby my feet get, I'm not doing that.

4. A hippo spins its tail like a propeller to splatter its poo in all directions. Apparently this spreads the nutrients from the poo into the water and helps the ecosystem. Frankly I'd swim well clear of any hippos.

5. Certain spiders disguise themselves as bird poo to avoid being eaten. Doesn't seem much of a life to me.

Still, at least knowing that all animals poo differently, and some can hold on to it for longer than others, reassured me that Zing was probably OK, though I'd still keep an eye on him. I just hoped there were no dragons that behaved like hippos!

The next few days actually turned out to be quite a lot of fun. Zing was making things hectic for me by crashing around everywhere and creating a ton of mess. But with Aura and Rosebud along for the ride, things just felt better.

They were also helping to distract me from my worries about the seedlings. And my frustration at having to call a halt to the search for Arturo's letters.

Although I tried to think of possible places Elvi could have hidden things, tapping walls and keeping my ears pricked for creaky floorboards, I really needed the superhero squad's help to carry on the search properly. But that would have to wait till the holiday was over.

We also found that Rosebud was a great help in the garden. Grandad and Jim were busy growing things to decorate the village. 'To give the place a bit of winter colour,' Grandad said, 'and us some practice for the Village in Bloom show in the spring.'

Not many flowers liked the colder months, but the few that did got a helping hand from Rosebud. We discovered that she could breathe orangey smoke that would make everything bloom.

'Do you think this little one might hang about?' Grandad said one afternoon, admiring some dragon-enhanced hellebores. 'I mean, I know these days you're extra careful to make sure all the dragons fly off, but I'm just saying, if this one wanted to stay on, just for a little while . . .'

He nodded at Zing. 'I see he's still hanging about too.'

'I have tried,' I said. 'I've been bringing him to the tree and showing him the other dragons flying off, but he just keeps coming back.'

'I expect he'll get the idea soon enough. Although maybe try and keep him away from our willow arch. Old Jim's been working on it for months. Star of our show, that thing.'

I wasn't sure I could promise anything when it came to Zing. But I smiled and nodded.

29
Singing Penguins and Remote-Controlled Dragons

On Wednesday Dad dropped me and Lolli at Nana and Grandad's, and Aura bounded in shortly after.

'So, Chipstick, I need a trip to the garden centre,' Grandad said. 'Anyone up for keeping me company? I expect we might find an ice cream along the way.'

I looked over at Aura, who grinned and nodded.

'Sure,' I said.

'Good-oh,' Grandad said. 'We'd best get a wriggle on then.'

He unpeeled Lolli, who was clinging to him and

waving a very happy-looking Stefan, wobbly felt-tip smile stretched wide.

'I wanna go with Guppie,' Lolli said. 'Lolly for Lolli.'

'You and me have got some fairy cakes to bake,' Nana said. 'Who's going to sprinkle all the sprinkles if you go rushing out?'

At the mention of sprinkles Lolli's eyes lit up, and Stefan twirled round equally happy.

As we made for the door, Grandad raised his eyebrows at the rucksacks Aura and I were hugging.

'Looks like someone's already got their wriggle on,' he said, motioning to my bag. He checked down the hall and lowered his voice. 'Is that really a good idea? You don't think it'd be better to leave your . . . "friends" here?'

'I think it's better to have them where we can keep an eye on them,' I said.

'They'll be no problem, honest,' Aura added, giving Grandad a beaming smile. She really was very good at the 'butter wouldn't melt and I've got everything under control' look.

'Right you are,' Grandad said, turning his gaze back on me. 'But let's keep this trip nice and short.'

Half an hour later we turned into the car park of a huge warehouse-like building.

'I just need to pick up some trellis panels. They've got all sorts here.'

'Including singing penguins on a sleigh,' Aura said, pointing out the window.

'Yup, including penguins,' Grandad chortled.

He wasn't wrong. The building itself was huge, and Christmas had definitely come early here. The whole of the front of the shop was festooned with trees and glitter and giant snowmen. Once we'd got through the sprawling Christmas display, there was a pet shop, an arts and craft area, toys, clothes, kitchenware, books and a very busy cafe.

'Come on, let's have a look around,' Aura said, pulling me towards a sign that said 'Pets'.

'I'll be out the back,' Grandad said. 'Just . . . you know . . . keep things under control.'

'Absolutely,' Aura said, giving him a massive thumbs up. 'We'll blend in like chameleons. And be as quiet as mice to boot.'

But of course we didn't do either of those things. Not once the dragons got loose.

I was just peering in at a particularly pretty corn snake when Aura came hurrying over.

'OK, so don't be cross and don't panic,' she hissed.

My heart sank.

'What have you done?'

'Me, nothing,' she said. 'But Rosebud might have decided to liberate some of the residents.'

I stared at her, and then dodged out the way as a woman with long curly hair rushed past, hands bashing at her head.

'It's on me! Get it off! Get it off!' she shrieked.

Aura dived forward managing to catch a mouse as the woman's hand flung it from her head.

'Still not panicking, please,' Aura said, seeing my stricken face. 'I only let Rosebud out to get some air. I saw all those birds cooped up in their cages and I didn't want her to feel like that. I guess you had the same idea about Zing,' she added, pointing up to the top of the fish tanks where Zing was whizzing back and forth.

'No, I didn't,' I said desperately. I grabbed my rucksack and saw the hole in the bottom. 'He must have bitten his way out.'

'It's fine,' Aura said quickly. 'We've got ash with us. They'll soon come back.'

I was about to say that Zing hadn't exactly shown much interest in ash and I doubted he'd start now there was so much else to catch his attention, when I noticed Aura looking around.

'Just as soon as I find Rosebud,' she muttered.

'You mean you don't know where she is?' I squeaked.

'It's fine. No one ever looks up. We'll soon have them tucked away safely again.'

'You don't know how much damage they can do.' I stood there in a daze, imagining the dragons igniting Christmas trees, scorching penguins and unleashing poo missiles. Aura grabbed my sleeve, shaking me out of it.

'No time for panic,' she said.

She was right. Zing hadn't loitered by the fish. He'd already decided to move on to the toys, landing on a shelf of remote-control cars. A little girl was standing with one of the controllers, her tongue poking out in a look of intense concentration as she tried to manoeuvre a sports car around her baby brother. It kept bashing into him and making him cry, at which point her mum grabbed the car and put it upside down

on a high shelf. Zing hopped from car to car along the shelf, the silver threads on his wings and body flaring as he moved from one to another.

Then he fluttered down to a lower shelf and, to my horror, the girl's arm stretched out and she grabbed hold of him! She dumped him on the floor and then bashed at the remote control again, as if it would make him fly. She squealed with delight as he rose up and started careering around above her.

'Look, Mummy!' she cried happily. 'I can do it.'

Her mother glanced up just as Zing dived down at super-speed. She yelped and covered her head and the baby's, but thankfully Zing swerved at the last second and zoomed off again, although weirdly he seemed to be pulling the woman's long black hair with him. It stuck up on end, as if someone had rubbed a balloon against her head.

As the woman grabbed the wailing girl, baby and buggy and retreated from the shop, Zing landed on a giant speaking teddy bear. I caught him and bundled him into my rucksack.

'I love you,' the teddy babbled happily.

I wasn't sure it would love Zing quite as much once it realised its bottom was smouldering. I hastily batted out the glowing sparks and hurried away.

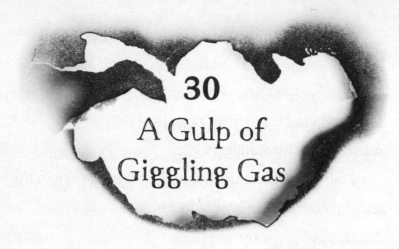

30
A Gulp of
Giggling Gas

Now I had to track down Aura. I just hoped she'd managed to find and catch Rosebud.

I eventually spotted her outside with all the garden pots and plants. I sped through the double doors and she hurried over to me.

'Isn't it amazing?' she said.

'Isn't what amazing?'

'All this,' she replied. And swept her hand at the tables laden with colourful flowers.

'Yeah, great. Flowers,' I said. 'But have you got her?'

'Don't worry, she's over there,' Aura said. 'But you don't get it. This was all her, Tomas. Nothing was in flower until she came. She flew over them, and it was like they all lifted their heads and bloomed in wonder at her. It was incredible.'

I felt my breathing slow and let myself take in the sea of colours. It really was incredible.

'People don't see anything,' Aura scoffed crossly. 'They're far too busy. No one has even batted an eyelid at all this.'

'I guess it's like Grandad always says. People don't actually want to see this sort of stuff, so generally they don't. It's easier not to.'

'They don't know what they're missing,' she said.

'It's probably a good thing,' I hissed, pointing at Rosebud. 'I think she just did a poo. It landed in the flower pot that man's just put in his trolley.'

He headed off, dragging it behind him.

'We have to get it back,' Aura cried. 'Her poos dry out really quickly. It'll explode in there!'

But we were already too late. The next second the poo detonated and the yellow-flowering plant from the pot rocketed out of the trolley. It shot up into the air, arced over a display of garden ornaments and landed upside down on a gnome's head, much to the surprise and obvious delight of a little boy in a pushchair.

Aura reached into her pocket and pulled out a handful of ash and, quick as a flash, Rosebud flitted down to her.

'Come on – let's go and find Grandad and get out of here,' I said. 'Before she unleashes another one!'

Finding Grandad still choosing trellis, we decided to keep a low profile behind some wooden pallets. Aura held Rosebud and gently stroked her green wings. As she did, the little dragon gave a shudder and a puff of green appeared from her back end.

'Did she just fart?' I said.

Aura laughed. 'I think so. She'd be fine here,' she added. 'Perfect camouflage for a garden centre.'

'I'm not sure curling up to look like a bud would be much use next to a glittery singing penguin or an inflatable Santa,' I pointed out.

'No, maybe not,' Aura laughed. 'This place smells amazing though, with all those flowers in full bloom.'

'It's weird that we can smell them way over here though,' I said.

'Actually, you know what?' Aura replied. 'I don't think it's the flowers. I think it's Rosebud.'

Unlike the Tyrannodragon Liam had unleashed, which emitted green gas rank enough it could shrivel living things, Rosebud's green gas was so sweetly scented it made you giddy. So giddy in fact that we soon found ourselves giggling uncontrollably.

'Did you see that woman's face?' Aura snorted. 'When she had that mouse in her hair.'

I howled, remembering. 'Well, you should have seen the mother of that little girl. Her hair stuck up on end so much she looked like a cartoon character who'd been electrocuted.'

I opened my rucksack and peered in at Zing who was now safely tucked into a section with no holes. Still chuckling, I reached down to scratch his horns, and quickly pulled my hand away with a yelp.

'He bit me,' I cried out, sucking on my finger but still laughing.

Aura, who was trying to look concerned, but failing to smother her giggles, nearly fell over backwards when she looked at me again. She snorted so loudly it made me crack up too.

'What is it?' I said, tears streaming down my face.

But Aura couldn't speak she was laughing so much. Eventually she squeaked: 'Your hair.'

I stood up and looked in the window of the summerhouse. And I shrieked with laughter at the grinning face looking back, hair sticking up on end.

31
Hola, Aurita!

Over the next couple of days we had a lot of fun with the dragons, especially thanks to Rosebud's ability to reduce people to giggling wrecks with one tiny sweetly scented fart. I had a feeling she knew exactly when to use her skills for maximum effect. Not only that, but Aura also proved pretty helpful when it came to the dragon-fruit tree. The next crop had ripened much faster than I expected and as the week went on, we had more dragons hatching out in the garden.

On Friday, as we sat on the bench watching Zing and Rosebud darting in and out of the leaves of the dragon-fruit tree, Aura said, 'Do you want to come over to mine for tea? Papi's making home-made tortillas with chicken pepián and his special guacamole. It's delicious.'

'OK,' I said.

I didn't know what pepián was and I'd never tried guacamole, but Aura seemed pretty confident I'd like them. Besides, thanks to Mum's attempts at puddings, I knew how to smile and chew. Even if swallowing sometimes took a leap of courage.

'Great,' she said. And she leaned closer. 'There's something I want to show you.'

Aura's house was bigger than ours, but it felt smaller. Probably because it was so full of stuff.

'My parents like to collect things,' Aura said, expertly rescuing me from falling flat on my face, as I nearly tripped over the elephant in the hallway.

'She's from India,' she said, bending down to pat the elephant's trunk. 'There's another one upstairs. In fact, there's probably a whole herd somewhere in here.'

She led me through the hall, where brightly coloured fabrics lined the walls, to the kitchen, where we found Aura's dad sitting at the table, his head buried in a book, one hand absently squeezing limes.

He had dark brown hair, like Aura's. Except his was neater. Aura's, I'd noticed, always seemed a bit preoccupied, like it was trying to find the best way off her head. A bit like mine, in fact.

'Hey, Papi,' Aura said picking up a slice of red pepper from the table and popping it into her mouth. 'This is Tomas.'

'*Hola*, Tomas, *hola*, Aurita,' he said. 'I'm afraid tea'll be a bit late. You can blame Professor Diaz.' He waved the book at us. 'Oh, and Mamma's got to teach this evening so it's just us three.'

He lifted a tea towel to reveal a tower of freshly made tortillas and handed us one each.

'Have one of these to keep you going.'

'Thanks,' we chorused.

'We'll be upstairs,' Aura said. Then she added, 'By the way, if you hear any bangs or crashes, don't worry. Tomas is a bit clumsy – he's always falling over stuff.'

I looked at her a bit shocked, but then she tipped her head very slightly towards the rucksack that I was cradling and I caught on. She was just thinking about Zing.

We made our way upstairs, squeezing past some boxes that had been left halfway up. I noticed the walls were full of photos of seascapes and cityscapes, mountains, forests and long sandy beaches. There was even one of her parents standing somewhere that looked very like the landscape of Jurassic World.

'So do you travel a lot?'

Aura glanced up at the pictures. 'Me? Nah. But my parents have. Mamma grew up here but she's been all over the world. She spent a lot of time in Mexico, because that's where my *abuelo* – my grandfather –

came from. That's where she met Papi too. He's from Guatemala but Mamma bumped into him when he was travelling around Mexico. I mean, she actually bumped into him, running around a corner. After that they taught and travelled – China, Japan, Thailand, lots of places in between, and then New Zealand. That's where I was born.'

'Wow,' I said. 'The furthest I've ever been is Cornwall.'

'I don't remember it,' she said with a shrug. 'We left when I was really little. But Mamma and Papi have been saving up ever since we moved back to England, so we can all go on our "grand adventure" – they're going to take me out of school for a year and teach me themselves while we travel the *whole* world.'

She was suddenly buzzing again, her eyes bright and twinkling. I wasn't sure if this was one of Aura's slight exaggerations, like when she said she knew everything about dragons. But somehow I didn't think so.

'Come on,' she urged. 'I want to show you Rosebud's garden.'

32
Nobody Likes
Jam Kippers

Aura definitely *hadn't* been exaggerating when it came
to how much she loved dragons. I stared around at
the themed bedspread and the books littering the
floor, the paper dragon lampshade flying above our
heads and the posters of dragons pinned between the
bright wall hangings. There were dozens of her own
sketches too and I peered at a few. They were mostly
pictures of the same dragon – a huge rose-pink one,
with four wings like a dragonfly, unleashing a burst
of rainbow flames. Aura saw where I was looking and
her hand shot out and tore the picture down, nearly

bringing the wall hanging next to it down too.

'Don't look at those,' she said. 'That was before I met you and found out dragons weren't just dreamed up in my head. Now, thanks to you, I *know* dragons don't have four wings.'

'Just because I've never seen a dragon with four wings, doesn't mean there couldn't be one,' I said quickly, not wanting her to rip down any more of her drawings. 'Every one I've seen has been different.'

She looked at the picture. 'I don't need to dream about dragons now. I've got one right here.'

Walking into Aura's room was also a bit like venturing into one of the glasshouses at the botanic garden. Everywhere I looked there were plants in pots, all shapes from wide glossy leaves, to frilled, spiky and even palms.

'I'm guessing Rosebud feels right at home,' I said.

Aura was at the window now. She'd pulled it open, and was dangling one leg over the sill. She beckoned me over. A little railed balcony stuck out from the wall,

just big enough to stand on. Although there was hardly room to stand as it was covered in even more plants.

'My *amma* loved gardening,' she replied. 'That's my granny,' she explained. She smiled, but it was a bit of a wobbly one. 'I think she'd have liked your grandad.'

I smiled too and leaned in to smell one of the flowers.

'I guess I got my green fingers from her,' she went on. 'Which is why all the plants are in my room – I'm like the rescue centre for neglected greenery.' She laughed.

I had an idea. 'Maybe you can help me with something,' I said. And I quickly explained about the dragon-fruit seedlings and how I was struggling to keep them alive, let alone get them to thrive.

'I'd be happy to take a look,' she said eagerly. 'How about I come round tomorrow?'

I grinned. 'You're on.'

Suddenly a leaf unfurled and Rosebud detached herself from one of the plants and fluttered onto Aura's outstretched hand. She stared down at the little dragon, her head tilting from side to side in time with the dragon's.

'Perhaps you should let Zing out for a fly,' she said. 'I'm surprised you've managed to get him to stay in your bag this long.'

She had a point.

'He's been sleepy all day,' I said, as I opened the bag and peered in, finding him still lying curled up at the bottom.

'Maybe he's just worn out,' Aura said. 'Or hungry.'

I lifted him out and laid him carefully on Aura's bed. 'I just wish I knew what he likes to eat,' I said. 'I hate not being able to look after him properly.'

Zing stretched his wings slowly and hopped half-heartedly along the bed and up onto the headboard. He turned his head, as if he was scanning the room for something. Then suddenly he launched forward,

tumbling rather than flying, and landed in a basket by the door that was overflowing with clothes.

He started burrowing into the clothes, until all we could see was the zigzag tip of his tail. Aura ran forward and hastily grabbed a pair of pants that Zing had flung out when he landed.

'What on earth's he doing?' she said.

Zing was thrashing about now in the laundry basket, sending socks and another pair of pants flying. Every so often his head or one wing would appear before vanishing again. The basket started to rock as the clothes were tossed and churned. Finally the rocking stopped and Zing hopped onto the rim of the basket. His sapphire eye was sparkling and the silver threads on his wings flared brightly.

If I'd been a cartoon character, at that moment a light bulb would have flared just as brightly above my head.

'Zapow!' I shrieked, making Aura jump in alarm. 'I think I finally understand why Zing doesn't like jam kippers.'

'I don't think anyone likes jam kippers,' Aura replied. 'And anyway, isn't it "Eureka", not "Zapow"?'

I laughed. 'Lolli had the answer all the time. Remember when I thought Zing had bitten me. All my hair stood on end, didn't it? What if it wasn't a bite? What if it was like a little electric shock? Like when you walk on a carpet and then touch something and get a zap.' I suddenly pictured the woman at the garden centre and also Mum, Dad and Lolli with their hair on end.

'You mean static electricity?'

'Exactly! What if he doesn't eat like the other dragons? What if he's actually charging up like a battery?'

Aura looked back at the laundry basket.

'You do get static from rubbing material,' she said.

'I'd always thought he was just having trouble sorting out his massive wings, but maybe he was actually charging himself up on the carpet. And he's always wriggling about in that pile of jumpers and socks under my bed.'

'Hang on, let's see if you're right,' she said excitedly. 'Woolly jumpers are the best things for static, aren't they?'

She rummaged in her cupboard and flung various things in my direction. I made a cosy nest for Zing and lowered him into it. He wriggled down into the material, and then wriggled some more. With every movement, the silver threads on his back and wings flared a little brighter. And then brighter. His wriggling sped up. Then suddenly he launched up into the air like a miniature rocket.

He started zipping around the room and in and out of the window over the little balcony of flowers. Then he circled back around and landed on the table next to Aura's bed. He hopped onto the radio alarm clock, which buzzed and blared out a few bars of a pop song before suddenly cutting out.

As Zing sped over to Aura's hairdryer, I let out another 'Zapow!'.

'That's why at the garden centre he raced right

over to all those remote-control toys. He must have been draining their charge, sucking on them like we suck on a sweet.'

The hairdryer Zing was perching on blasted out hot air and then with a fizzle abruptly stopped working.

'And that must be why the TV blew and Dad's been having problems with the food mixer and the other electrics in the house. It's all been Zing!'

'I guess this is his equivalent of being let loose in a sweet shop!' Aura laughed as Zing spotted a remote-controlled helicopter on her toy shelf.

Zing's scales shone electric blue and the silver threads along his body pulsed. The air began to crackle around him. And then, without warning, what looked like a mini lightning bolt shot out of his open mouth.

33
Shining a Spotlight

The bolt made a fair-sized scorch mark on a patch of Aura's carpet.

'Wow! Did he just belch lightning?!'

'I think so!' I cried. 'He's never done *that* before.'

'Maybe he just needed to let one out, like a burp,' Aura giggled.

Zing launched up into the air and started zipping back and forth above us. Let's just say it was a good job Aura had told her dad not to worry about bangs and crashes. There was a lot of stuff to avoid in Aura's room, and Zing wasn't missing anything!

He seemed to be getting faster and faster at flying too. We only had to turn our backs for a second, usually to check one of the mini lightning bolts hadn't actually burned a hole in anything, to find he'd disappeared and was perching on a shelf at the other side of the room.

Rosebud's little puffs of green fart didn't help. In fact they seemed to send Zing into even more dizzying aerial acrobatics.

When Aura's dad called up the stairs that tea was ready, I was mid-dive, an arm outstretched to catch a photo Zing had just knocked off Aura's wall.

'Good save,' Aura said with obvious relief. 'I'd hate that to get zapped by lightning. It's too precious.'

I glanced at the picture before handing it to her.

'That's my *abuelo*, Miguel, outside his family's house in Mexico. He died when Mamma was about my age so I never met him. We don't have many pictures of him.'

Putting the photo safely out of harm's way, we quickly tidied up anything Zing might use to charge himself up.

'Do you think he'll be OK while we go and have tea?' she asked, looking nervously at the chaos he'd already unleashed on her room.

'How fast can you eat?' I said.

As it turned out we could both eat super-fast. Probably because her dad was a really good cook and she had been absolutely right about the food being delicious.

 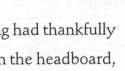

When we got back to Aura's room, Zing had thankfully settled down. Rosebud was perched on the headboard, peering at him, while he lay curled on Aura's pillow.

We sat cross-legged on the floor, drinking steaming mugs of hot chocolate, and started leafing through the many books Aura had collected. As I downed the last mouthful, a little dragon stared back at me. It was curled around the bottom of the inside of the mug, like the dragon in the pot in Grandad's shed, the one he kept his gardening bits in.

'You really do like dragons,' I said, waving the mug at her.

She grinned back, wiping the chocolate from her lips.

Rosebud fluttered over and landed on her leg. The little dragon stretched herself out, and wrapped her wings around Aura's knee, clinging to her. After a minute Zing lifted his head and, seeing us, flew over and landed – with a slightly undignified bump – in my lap. He turned in little circles for a while, but couldn't seem to get himself, or his massive wings, comfy. And his claws were treading painfully into my legs, making me wriggle too.

I thought he'd given up when he launched back into the air, but then he flew round behind me and landed on my back. My jumper pulled as he clawed himself higher. Eventually he stretched out his wings so that they lay across the top of my shoulders and his head, tipped to one side, rested over my neck. And that's where he stayed, quite happily. Moving gently up and down as I breathed.

On the way home, Zing flitted from street lamp to street lamp above me. He flew ahead and paused on each one, timing it just right so that as I reached it, the lamp flared brightly. It was as if I was walking out onto a stage and he was there waiting to shine a spotlight on me.

When I lay in bed that night, Zing making the air around me crackle, I dreamed of playing with him in

Grandad's garden, among the other hatching dragons; running between the fruit trees, bare feet on grass, warm under the sun; laughing as he darted between branches, disappearing and then reappearing to ambush me.

When I woke from the dream in the morning and discovered Zing had wriggled in next to my feet, I couldn't help smiling.

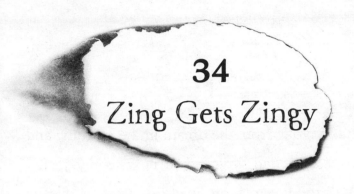

34
Zing Gets Zingy

After a good sleep and with renewed hope that Aura would be able to offer some advice when she came over later, I jumped out of bed to shower the seedlings with worm poo. As my hand reached for the bag though, I felt my stomach drop.

'Oh no,' I whispered.

I grabbed the first little pot and desperately tried to prop up the withered seedling it contained. My eyes raced to the next one. It was also lying forlorn and shrivelled. One by one I took them all in, desperation rising through me in a great whoosh that threatened

to blast all the hair off my head. Eleven pots. Eleven shrivelled dragon-fruit plants. They were all dead. Not one single seedling had survived.

I needed Aura. Maybe they just looked dead, and she – or even Rosebud – could do something to revive them?

I charged down the hall and barrelled into Lolli's room. 'Lolli, I need to go and get Aura right now. Can you keep an eye on Zing for me?'

She nodded fiercely and then stood to attention, giving me a salute that nearly poked her eye out. 'I make him some bekkiefast if he wakes up.'

I quickly explained about Zing's unusual eating habits and the way he was charging himself up.

Lolli gave me a double thumbs up with extra waggling.

'Thanks, Lolli, you're a star.'

When I came back with Aura in tow, I knew something was wrong as soon as I opened the front door. We were met by a cacophony of sound, throbbing music from the radio, blaring voices from the TV, the hoover revving up, a whirring food mixer squealing from the kitchen and Dad's recording equipment making a very strange whistling noise.

Dad was standing in the hall, looking alarmed, holding his buzzing electric razor at arm's length, as though he thought it might leap out of his hand and start attacking his face. Meanwhile Mum was running round switching all the lights off.

'Quick, Tomas, before any more blow,' she said. 'The electrics have gone haywire!'

Aura and I hurried round flicking switches on sockets. Out of the corner of my eye I saw a nervous-looking Lolli on the stairs.

Her hair was sticking up at an outrageous angle. And she wasn't the only one. She was cradling Mr Floppybobbington, the fluffy bunny she'd been helping Mum look after, and he now looked like a giant white pompom with a tiny pink nose.

I raced over. 'Lolli,' I hissed. 'What's happening?'

'I'm sorry,' she said. 'Zing woke up really, *really* hungry. He rolled in my dressing gown, and then he got all happy and zingy at the lemons.'

She held up a bag full of the remains of about a dozen lemons that had been sucked dry. She looked at them, obviously confused.

'Citric acid,' I muttered,

remembering a science experiment I'd done once with Grandad where we'd made a battery out of a lemon. Of course he'd love lemons.

'And then . . .' Lolli went on. 'He got in the big drawer of batteries. And got really extra twirly.'

I looked at Aura. 'I need to find Zing. Before my super-charged dragon blows up our whole house,' I said. 'Can you go up to my room and see what you can do with the seedlings?'

I'd told Aura about them on our way back and she didn't need asking twice. She raced up the stairs while I followed Lolli into the kitchen, leaving Mum and Dad to wrestle the household appliances in the lounge.

'I opened the door,' Lolli said, peering outside. 'Will Zing be OK?'

Her bottom lip had started to go all wibbly-wobbly and tears were rolling down her cheeks, splashing onto Mr Floppybobbington's fluffed-up fur.

I gave her a squeeze and my best 'everything's going to be OK' smile.

'He'll be fine, Lollibob. You did the right thing. I'm sure he'll zoom it off and soon calm down.'

To be honest I wasn't sure at all, but I gave her another hopeful smile.

'Am I still the bestest vetninarin in the whole wide world?'

'The very bestest,' I said. 'A veterinarian extraordinaire,' I replied, stumbling a bit over the word myself.

She sniffed and wiped her nose on Mr Floppy-bobbington, who didn't seem to mind, which probably went to show just what a good vet she actually was.

Aura ran into the kitchen and skidded on a lemon rind.

'I'm sorry, Tomas,' she said as she slid towards us.

I grabbed hold of her arm and steadied her.

'They're too far gone,' she said breathlessly. 'I don't think there's anything we can do to bring them back.'

35
Follow That Dragon!

This was the worst news.

'Are you sure?' I asked.

Aura nodded sadly.

'I can't believe I've killed them all,' I moaned. 'What are the others going to say? They trusted me to look after them.'

'It's OK,' Aura said.

But it really wasn't.

Thoughts started whizzing like exploding popcorn in my head. One of the popcorn grains – the one that contained the 'What if Flicker doesn't come back?'

question – had sizzled and burnt into a hard black kernel. Despite all the excitement with Zing and Aura, that one had been lying in the pan smouldering for the last week.

'If the big dragons never come back, there'll be no Maxi to breathe on any more seeds. These could have been the last active trees. The dragons need them – they needed me to keep them safe,' I said miserably.

'We can go and look for some more,' Aura said. 'It'll be easier with two of us.'

I emitted a strange squeak in an attempt to hold back some of Lolli's wibbly-wobbliness that had attached itself to me, and she hastily added, 'Right now if you like.'

'What about Zing?' I said. 'I can't leave him charged up like this.'

Aura pointed through the door to the garden. And I was relieved to see the little sky-blue dragon, whizzing back and forth, skimming across the grass.

'I'm sure he'll follow,' she said.

As we hurried down the road, Zing did follow, speeding from tree to tree above us, darting ahead and then shooting back. Every so often he would pause on a street light. When that happened there was a burst of orange that got brighter and brighter until the bulb shattered and Zing zoomed off again. He wouldn't be calming down at this rate.

Once at the botanic garden, we raced through the gates, me holding out my entrance pass and Aura waving a Top Trumps card with a baby hippo on it. Thankfully, as usual, the girl had her head in a book and didn't even register we were there. Feet skidding on the gravel, we ran on along the path.

'Do you think he'll be OK out here?' I said, motioning to Zing, who was zipping around madly between the trees.

'Better off out here than in there,' Aura said, nodding at the glasshouse. 'And there are no more street lamps, so hopefully he'll wear himself out a bit.'

She looked about as convinced as I had when I'd

said the same thing to Lolli. But we didn't have any choice. There was no way we'd catch him at the speed he was flying, and as usual my little handful of ash was doing nothing to entice him. Luckily Rosebud was happy to curl up inside Aura's jacket, with her wings folded over and her head tucked away.

'Right, let's start this end and work our way down,' I said when we were safely inside the glasshouse. 'Be careful no one sees you sneaking off the path.'

Aura nodded and gave me a rallying smile and we set to it. But after an hour of crawling through the undergrowth, I had to admit defeat.

'Come on, Tomas. I'm not giving up and neither are you,' Aura declared. 'We just need a Plan B.'

She reminded me of Kat and Kai, who were always coming up with plans. Sometimes we went through so many plans we ended up with a Plan F and once even a Plan P!

As Aura bundled me along the path and out of the automatic doors, I saw Zing zooming over the roof of the glasshouse, heading in the opposite direction. He still hadn't slowed down.

'I can't leave him here all supercharged up,' I said. 'We'd better try to see where he's gone.'

Hurrying around the front of the glasshouse, we spotted him flying through a copse of trees. We followed, winding our way through, trying to keep the little dragon in sight. Eventually we stumbled out onto a path. To the right it led through a bamboo arch, where I spied the ornamental pond beyond. And to the left, a gate and the courtyard garden of an old cottage. It was a bit like something out of a fairy tale, with timbers on the outside and old diamond-shaped window panes. I'd seen it before when I'd been exploring with Lolli. Dad said it was probably used by the head gardener once upon a time, but he didn't think anyone lived there now. Running alongside one wall I could see two long greenhouses nestled side by side, their pitched roofs glinting in the sunshine. But Zing was nowhere in sight.

Ahead of us on the path a family huddled together, filling in one of the botanic garden quiz sheets.

'Where did he disappear to?' Aura whispered, looking around frantically.

A little boy in a pushchair was jiggling madly and pointing in the direction of the house.

'Daga daga daga,' he babbled.

'This way,' I said, and gave the boy a thumbs up.

Racing towards the house, we both skidded to a halt as someone stepped out of the trees onto the path.

'Hello, Tomas. Exploring again? Nice to see you keeping to the paths this time. And with a friend, I see.' Chouko smiled at Aura.

I opened my mouth to reply, but at that moment I saw what Chouko was cradling under her arm. Instead of actual words, what came out sounded like a baby goat stepping on a drawing pin.

Aura looked as surprised as Chouko at my bleat, especially when I started trying to tell her what I'd seen using some bizarre eyebrow-based semaphore.

Luckily Aura could read eyebrow, and her gaze shot to the little pot. And the dragon-fruit seedling it contained!

'I'm Aura,' she said quickly, stepping in. 'Tomas is showing me around, because I love plants and growing things and I'm interested in tropical plants especially and it's so cool here because you have all sorts of things from all over the world and I wish I had a glasshouse like this but I've just got a balcony although it's crammed full and it's great because I get bees and butterflies . . .' Aura finally ran out of breath.

'My name means butterfly,' Chouko said softly, a warm smile spreading across her face. 'And I am just like you. I love plants and I love this place. But you'll have to excuse me for a moment as I need to get this little one tucked up in the warm.' She looked down at the pot with the dragon-fruit seedling and smiled at it as if it was a little kitten asleep in her arms.

Then she turned and unlatched the gate to the cottage, making the sign that read 'Private' wobble and rattle.

36
A Supercharged Stink

'We have to get it back,' I hissed.

'I know,' Aura replied. 'But we need to be careful. We don't want to get banned from the botanic garden. We need to pause and think.'

'We don't have time to pause and think,' I groaned. 'Look where Zing is!'

Aura followed the line of my finger. Her hand shot to her mouth and her eyes widened in alarm. Somehow Zing had got into the outer greenhouse and was whizzing back and forth inside. I could see Chouko in the one that adjoined the house, leaning over a bench to tend to some pots. If she turned to look into the other greenhouse, she would see him.

'What if she goes in there next?' Aura squeaked.

'Then Chouko might see her very first dragon,' I said, 'and that would not be good.'

'We have to get him out. How did he even get in there?'

'Look,' I said pointing up to the roof. 'There's a skylight open – he must have flown in there. I just need to get in and guide him out. There are doors at the back. You'll have to distract Chouko so I can get round unseen.'

'OK,' Aura said. 'Let's go.'

While Chouko was poring over some plants with her back to us, Aura pushed open the gate and we hurried down the path. Luckily the greenhouses had a low brick base below the glass panels. So I was able to crawl on my hands and knees to the back door, while Aura creaked open the door to the first greenhouse.

'Excuse me,' I heard her say.

I didn't wait to hear what elaborate ruse Aura had come up with. As I pushed open the back door of the greenhouse, I winced. Zing had knocked so many pots flying that there was soil and uprooted plants littering the floor everywhere. He was crashing around under the counters and then he began swiping his tail across a pile of felt-like material, the sort Grandad used to protect plants from frost.

'Don't start charging up now,' I pleaded.

Seeing me, the little dragon just swiped harder.

The air crackled and then he let out a lightning bolt that scorched a gardening glove.

'Why are you making things worse?' I said, exasperated.

Flicker had always helped when we'd got into sticky situations. But Zing was just adding frenzy to the chaos.

More mini lightning bolts zapped out of his mouth in every direction. And I could see the threads across his wings sparking brilliant silver. I glanced into the other greenhouse and saw Aura and Chouko laughing. It looked as if Aura had had some help from one of Rosebud's giggly green farts. But then my heart plummeted as I saw Chouko stepping out of the greenhouse.

A confused look passed over Chouko's face as she turned the handle of the door and saw me through the glass. She looked back at Aura, who attempted to smile, but it just crumbled into pieces on her face.

Desperately my eyes shot to Zing, who was hovering up by the skylight. I willed him to fly out through the open window. But he looked straight back at me and then rocketed downwards just as Chouko stepped inside. I sprang forward, convinced he was going to crash into her head.

But then the strangest thing happened. A blinding flash of light. So bright my eyes instinctively shut tight. As I opened them again I saw Chouko and Aura making the same screwed-up expressions.

'What's going on in here?' Chouko demanded.

Then her face properly fell as she lowered her hand. 'What have you done to all my specimens, and *what* is that terrible smell?'

37
Crash Bang Zing

I sniffed and caught a metallic tang in the air. It smelt like the time Dad had burned the wires in an old radio he was trying to fix.

Before I could answer, smoke started rising up, billowing from a climate-control unit beside me.

'I'm sorry,' I coughed through the smoke.

Without hesitating, Chouko dashed forward, pulled me to my feet and dragged me out of the greenhouse.

'Both of you, wait there,' she said quickly. 'I don't know what's going on, but I need to get a fire extinguisher before I lose everything, including my house.'

'Where's Zing?' Aura cried as Chouko hurried off.

I looked around, hoping he'd flown out the skylight. But there was no sign of him.

'Hold on,' Aura said, suddenly pointing to the other greenhouse, the one she and Chouko had first gone into. 'There he is!'

Zing was hovering at the back of the greenhouse above a small plastic polytunnel running along one counter – a polytunnel he was rapidly tearing to shreds.

'How on earth did he get in?' I cried.

'I don't know,' Aura said. 'But look what's under there.'

My eyes fell on the row of little pots, and the dragon-fruit tree seedlings poking out of each and every one.

I looked at Zing. He stared back at me, a piece of the polytunnel clutched in his claws. He'd been leading us to the dragon-fruit seedlings! Not trying to cause more trouble. He might not go about it in the same way as Flicker would have, but he'd been trying to help. I just hadn't realised. The truth was, I hadn't stopped to listen.

'I'm sorry,' I mouthed. I pointed at myself and then at him, and then joined my index finger and thumb on both hands and interlocked them. Using the sign language Miss Jelinski had taught us in class, I wanted him to know we were in this together.

'Chouko locked the greenhouse door,' Aura wailed. 'He can't get out. And she's going to come back any second and then she'll see him. She must know they are dragon-fruit trees she's growing. It won't take a mastermind to put two and two together and work out why you've been so fascinated by strange cacti.'

'What are we going to do?'

'I don't know, Tomas, I'm all out of plans. This is really bad.' Her hands were scratching at her hair, her eyes wide. 'I think it might be time to panic.'

Hearing Aura squeak the word 'panic' reminded me of her response to my own panicking in the garden centre. I took a breath. Zing needed me to stay calm.

The next second there was another brilliant flash of light. We shielded our eyes from the glare of the greenhouse.

'There's that weird smell again,' Aura said. 'Like the smell you get before a storm.'

'Or lightning,' I added slowly.

We turned and saw a scorch mark on the grass beside us. And then our eyes fell on Zing, hopping from foot to foot. He wasn't sky blue with silver threads any more – he was a dazzling brilliant white, lit up and flashing, the air crackling fiercely around him.

'Did he just do what I think he did?' I said. 'Did he just zap out of there?'

'You know we said he was as fast as lightning?' Aura said, a grin starting to spread across her face. 'Well, I think we were wrong. I think he *is* lightning.'

Zing cocked his head to the side and then flew up, circling above us. And for the first time his wings didn't flap awkwardly and he didn't look as if he would crash into anything.

I grinned up at him. One sapphire eye shone back. And for a split second, in the swirling cloud of the other eye, I saw the flash of a lightning bolt.

He landed on my back, his silver-white wings stretching out across my shoulders. I instinctively braced myself, thinking I'd get an electric shock, but all I felt was a wonderful tingling spreading down my arms and into my fingers. Like I was quietly buzzing with magic.

38
Time to Own Up

Aura and I hurried away, dizzy with relief and keen to put as much distance as possible between us and Chouko – and any questions she might fire our way. Rosebud unfurled from Aura's arm and flew up into the trees and Zing followed. They darted to and fro above us, chasing each other, Zing's scales shining white against the autumn leaves.

As we neared the gate, they both zipped down and disappeared into our jackets and tucked themselves safely out of sight. Not wanting to draw attention to ourselves, we did our best to saunter out onto the street. But as soon as we were past the entrance we fell into giggles and raced our way homewards.

'You look happier,' Mum said when she tucked me in.

I nodded and smiled, aware of Zing curled beneath my bed. By the time we'd got home, he'd returned to his usual sky blue. I'd settled him in his nest of clothes, laying my hand on his head and scratching his back as he watched me, his eyes shining brightly. Thanks to him, I knew there were more seedlings, which meant we still had a chance to get things right.

'I'm glad you've made a new friend,' she continued. 'Aura seems lovely. And you've got the rest of the superhero squad back tomorrow too. All is right with the world, hey?'

She left and turned out the light, and I lay there, my eyes wide open. A mouldy feeling had suddenly started growing inside my tummy.

With the superhero squad coming back, I had some owning up to do. I wondered how annoyed they would be at me for blurting out the secret to Aura. I tried and tried to figure out the right way to tell them, and the perfect time. But really there isn't ever a perfect time to admit you've done something wrong.

Grandad always says you just have to bite the bullet and do it anyway. Otherwise the mould will grow and grow and turn your insides furry.

Then I started picturing the hurt on Chouko's face when she'd seen the wreckage in her greenhouse. And I knew I needed to make things right with her too.

I lay there, unsure if I wanted to sleep, afraid my dreams might turn mouldy as well. Zing flapped out from under the bed and landed beside me, bashing me

in the head with one wing. The buzz that came from his little body had a weirdly calming effect this time. Like he was draining the wound-up worry energy I was storing inside.

I closed my eyes and let myself drift off.

In my dream I was standing on the craggy side of a mountain under a wild sky. Above me storm clouds buffeted each other like raging bulls. Lightning burst from them, jagged and bright, leaping from cloud to cloud in a dazzling electric dance.

And then one bolt shot straight at me. As the tip of it reached my outstretched hand, I thought I would be struck down. But the light burst into the shining white scales of a dragon.

The dragon settled across my shoulders and leaned his head against my neck. A blast of energy lit me up inside and I shone bright and luminous.

I was still buzzing with that energy when I woke up. Feeling revived by the dream, I summoned the superhero squad. And everyone agreed to meet later that day in Grandad's garden.

After helping Dad set up his microphone to record a very reluctant Tomtom and a super-friendly and very keen collie dog called Poppy Mobello Madonna, who Mum had just brought home, I took Lolli with me to Nana and Grandad's.

Aura was already there when we arrived, holding a plate of Nana's jammy tarts.

'Your nana has gone back for more,' she said, smiling.

I grabbed a raspberry tart and a blackberry one and stuffed them into my mouth, hoping their sweet stickiness would settle the fluttering butterflies in my tummy. The happy buzz of my dream was starting to wear off as the time to face the superhero squad grew ever closer.

While Aura and Rosebud helped Grandad with his flowers, and Zing helped by staying out of their way, I took out my worries on some nettles, watched over by Lolli. Her efforts with Stefan and the other sticky patients had finally been rewarded by Mum, who'd given her sole charge of Mr Floppybobbington. Although, to be fair, she still carried Stefan around with her.

'Hey up, Chipstick – looks like we've got a few more helping hands at last,' Grandad called.

I turned and, seeing the superhero squad heading down the garden path towards us, my heart leaped up and started thumping at my chest to get out.

As they got closer, I saw Rosebud curl her wings and retreat into bud stealth mode. I wished I had her skills! Even Aura was looking nervous now the time had come.

39
The Superhero Squad Forever

I braced myself for the laser-beam glares I was sure were about to be unleashed.

Everyone had their eyes fixed on Aura and the little shape clinging to her arm. But there were no glares.

When Zing careered across the path, letting out one of his mini lightning bolts, Ted actually grinned and called out, 'There he is! I told you he was zippy – although I had no idea he could do that!'

'Wow!' Liam cried. And Kai burst out laughing as Zing sent two more bolts shooting across the grass.

'He really is sparky,' Kat giggled.

And then Zing's scales shone white and with a flash of light he disappeared, only to reappear right next to Liam's head. Alarmed, Liam jumped and then started laughing as Zing zapped from him to Kai and back again.

'That's incredible!' Kai squealed as the dragon suddenly appeared right in front of him.

'We come in peace,' Liam hollered, spinning round, searching for the dragon.

Meanwhile, Kat rushed over to Aura. She started firing questions at her about the dragon on her arm.

'What's her name? Does she breathe fire? Why do her horns glow like that?'

'She's called Rosebud, because she curls up like a bud. And it's like my mamma's name,' Aura said happily.

Before she could go on, Kat turned and fired one at me: 'Tomas, why didn't you tell us Aura had found out?'

I shuffled awkwardly. Zing appeared next to me, and, to Liam and Kai's obvious relief, settled on my back, his wings stretching out across my shoulders.

'Because she didn't just find out,' I mumbled, scuffing the mud with the tip of my trainer.

'What do you mean?' she asked.

'I mean, I told her. Even though we said we wouldn't.'

Kat gave a little 'oh' of understanding, as the truth fell into place like counters lining up in a game of Connect Four.

'So?' Kai said matter-of-factly.

'Yeah. I was all for telling her anyway,' Liam pointed out.

'We would have told her sooner or later,' Ted said.

'Exactly,' Kat agreed.

Aura looked visibly relieved at hearing this.

'I shouldn't have done it without checking with everyone though,' I said apologetically. Then, feeling like I wanted to explain, I added, 'I just felt as if the superhero squad was falling apart. You've all been so busy. And then with Flicker staying away, and knowing you were going to be away for the holidays . . .

and that you two will be going off to the other side of the world . . . I just . . . I messed up. I'm sorry,' I finished lamely.

Kat looked at me, her head tipped slightly to one side, like Flicker sometimes did, as if I was a puzzle she was trying to figure out.

'It's fine,' she said softly. 'Honestly, I feel a whole lot better about going away knowing you have someone here to help you all while we're gone. You need her.'

'You sure do,' agreed Kai. 'Anyway, what do you mean about the superhero squad falling apart?'

'Yeah,' piped up Ted. 'What's that all about?'

I shrugged, feeling embarrassed. 'You're always off in Liam's allotment,' I said quietly. 'I guess I got a bit grumpy at being left out of your grand plans,' I finally admitted.

'I get it,' Liam said. 'Being left out makes you act weird. I should know.' He elbowed me and added in a deep and gruff voice, 'Don't turn out like me though, son.'

Aura giggled. And I couldn't help joining in as I felt my whole body untie itself from the bundle of knots it'd worked itself into over the last few weeks.

'Listen, I'm sure the dragons will come back,' Ted said. 'They know where we are.' Everyone nodded. 'We're all in this together, the dragons *and* us.'

'And it doesn't matter where we are in the world, Tomas,' Kai said earnestly, 'the superhero squad's greatest superpower is our super-strength stickiness. Not even the Hulk could pull us lot apart.'

The relief at hearing that threatened to leak out, but luckily Aura stepped in and distracted everyone. She quickly told them about our adventures in the botanic garden and Chouko finding the seedlings. By the time she'd finished, I was leak-free.

'We'll find a way to rescue the seedlings,' Ted said, giving me a reassuring nudge.

'Absolutely,' agreed Liam.

'And just because we'll be in China doesn't mean we can't help,' Kat said, and Kai added, 'Who else is going to come up with your cunning plans?'

'Actually Aura's pretty good at plans,' I said, smiling at her.

Kat linked arms with Aura. 'Excellent. Welcome to the planning committee!'

'Come on,' Grandad said, striding over and pulling out his phone. 'Let's have a snap of the superhero squad all together.'

We huddled in close and Grandad called out, 'Say: "Dragon-fruit tree"!'

It worked and we all grinned our way through an extra-long 'treeeeeee' as he clicked to take the picture. Then we fell about in a giggling heap when we saw that Zing's static had given us all wildly sticking-up hair – including the ever so fluffy Mr Floppybobbington.

40
A Buzz and a Flicker

Later, when everyone had gone home, I sat with Grandad on the bench outside the shed. Zing was perched on the end, the air crackling around him as tiny blue sparks jumped from spine to spine along his back.

He kept his bright sapphire eye fixed on me as he launched up into the air and began circling above our heads. Then he flew down to land on my back, where he wriggled his way up until he could rest his head over my shoulder. I smiled at the pulse of energy that buzzed through me. Then I stared down at the picture

Grandad had taken of us all with our grinning faces, arms across each other's shoulders.

Feeling the weight of Zing on my shoulder, I closed my eyes and leaned in to Grandad, my head suddenly full of thoughts of Flicker.

'Do you think Flicker will come back?'

'Why on earth shouldn't he?' asked Grandad.

'In my dreams now, it's always Zing and me playing.'

'He's a sparky little dragon, that's for sure,' Grandad chuckled.

'But it used to be me and Flicker.' And as I said the words, I felt the familiar stab in my heart. 'What if Flicker felt left out, like I did with Liam and Ted, and that's why he's been staying away?'

Grandad took the camera from me and smiled as he studied the picture. Then he held it up in front of me.

'Who's missing from this?' he said, pointing.

'What do you mean?' I asked, peering at it. 'No one's missing.'

'Yes, there is. Me.'

I wasn't sure what he was getting at.

'You know, Chipstick, not everyone gets to be in the photo,' he said. 'Unless you're using one of those silly sticks!'

He paused and squeezed me tighter.

'There's usually someone taking the picture. Someone who doesn't necessarily want to get in the way but is there keeping an eye, joining in on all those magic moments, even if it's off to one side.'

I thought of all the dreams I'd shared with Flicker, seeing the world through his eyes. And then I pictured all my dreams recently, swapped to scenes of me and Zing. In my dreams, I realised I was still seeing what Flicker saw.

'Just because he's not in the picture himself, doesn't mean he's not still there,' Grandad went on.

'I reckon he just thought you needed a bit of time and space to grow a few new friends.'

And just like that, as I sat tucked into Grandad's side, I felt like I was leaning against the warming scales of Flicker.

I knew then with total certainty that Grandad was right. Flicker didn't have to come back, because he hadn't gone anywhere, he'd always been there. Just off to one side, like Grandad.

And I couldn't wait until I saw him again.

Because when I did, I knew there would be adventures galore.

Of course, what I didn't know then was that Aura had a secret. A secret not even she knew about. But maybe if you've had your eyes wide open you've already worked it out.

If not, just you wait, because things are about to hot up!

Acknowledgements

This book simply wouldn't have made it into the world without my fabulous editor Georgia Murray. Georgia, I can't thank you enough for your belief in me and in this story. Your keen eye, kind guiding hand and unwavering faith saw us through. So thank you!

I'm so delighted that the wonderful Talya Baker has been a part of this editing magic again too – thank you for your careful attention to detail and knowing my characters so well. My thanks too to Hannah Featherstone for her expert eye with the proofreading.

A massive thank-you to the whole team at Piccadilly, who have got behind this series and still get so excited about my dragons. And to my lovely agent, Jo Williamson, for all her amazing support along the way.

Every time I get illustrations from Sara Ogilvie I give a squeal and this book is no exception. Thank you to the genius that is Sara, for giving us illustrations with such heart, tenderness and fun. And to Nick Stearn and Sue Michniewicz for their incredible design skills.

The dragons wouldn't be flying so high without the superhero squad of bloggers, reviewers, teachers, librarians and of course fabulous readers who have given the dragons a home. So many people have cheered me and the dragons on over the past few years, too many to name. But please know that every kind review and comment lifts our wings a little higher. So thank you from the bottom of our hearts!

I couldn't do any of this without my family and friends. Near and far, you have done so much to keep me going me in this mad malarkey of writing. You're a bonkers and wonderful lot!

And finally, heart-filled thanks to Ian, Ben and Jonas for endlessly cheering me on and filling my days with love and silliness. I'm proud of these books – I'm even prouder of you.